FATE OF THE CLIPPER *WESTWIND*

Fate of the
Clipper *Westwind*

JOHN SCOTT DOUGLAS

1954

Dodd, Mead & Company

NEW YORK

Contents

To Andrew Sanfilippo, Captain John Rippo, Captain John Tufts, Larry W. Holland, Captain Sam Crivello and many other friends of the tuna fleet for their generous help in supplying the author with countless details about the fishermen who sail thousands of miles in search of the roving schools of tuna, this book is respectfully dedicated

CHAPTER ONE

The Quest for the

Clipper *Westwind*

LEAVING THE noisy clanking and rattling of the cannery be-hind, Randy Draper stepped out onto the dock. The crisp, salty ocean breeze, blowing across Coronado Island and South San Diego Bay, was refreshingly cool after the warm, humid air of the plant.

Off to the right of the Italo-American Canning Company dock he saw a tuna boat discharging her catch. A crane, creaking raspingly, raised a big black hopper from a fish well in the boat's after-deck, swinging it to an overhead trough. Randy watched a worker on an elevated platform grasp and tip the rectangular container, to spill frozen fish into the flume. The boy could hear the *swish* of sea water sweeping the tuna along to a glassed-in room on another plat-form, high above him. Up there, he knew, a weighmaster and a crew member of the unloading boat would record the poundage of the fish before it flowed on into the plant.

The boat ridding herself of fish, however, was not the one he sought. So he passed her and another small, weather-beaten craft, walking with a slow, almost reluctant step.

Randy was large of frame, and in dungarees and open-necked shirt, with sleeves rolled above strong, brown fore-arms, he looked older than his seventeen years. Beneath the unruly curl of his close-cropped black hair his face showed the deep tan of desert sun and sea glare. His level gray eyes and wide mouth were usually touched with a humor that was missing now.

When he reached a larger boat, the *Ripple,* he stopped abruptly, the rugged contours of his face working in troubled lines. Memories of the many times he had romped from stem to stern of this vessel with Frank Castignoni crowded into his mind, and he shrank from another visit when his friend was not with him.

I've got to go aboard, he thought. I'll never find Frank unless I do! Still he stared at the boat with misted eyes, making no move.

She was a staunch vessel, known for her hundred-foot length as a "tuna clipper." The white paint of her raised forepeak, as well as the high wheelhouse and captain's cabin above it, gleamed blindingly in the brilliant California sunlight. She had the unique design that makes tuna boats unlike any other fishing craft. Her stern sat low, weighed down by eight deep wells sunk into her deck for the storage of Diesel oil or frozen fish. Aft of these wells additional weight was put upon the after-end by three huge, square boxes, the bait tanks. Uprights supported an open-sided wooden covering or canopy that would shield small fish in the tanks from direct sunlight. And on it stood the heavy chocks that cradled the scouting plane used in finding schools of tuna when the clipper was at sea. But the plane was not aboard now.

In his countless visits to the *Ripple* with the owner's son, Randy had come to regard her as a scientific marvel. Automatic devices, refrigerating machinery and miles of electrical wiring had created a boat of specialized design that might have been likened to a floating cold storage plant adapted for the pursuit of a single species of fish.

Yet to him the *Ripple* and her kind suggested romance and adventure as no other modern vessel could. A "hook-and-liner" on which men still pitted their strength against the fighting fury of great yellowfin tuna, she had sailed thousands of leagues over sunny seas in her searches for the roving schools of fish, much as the whalers of bygone days had hunted bowheads and cachalots. Her fishermen had heard her stout timbers wrenching in shrieking equatorial hurricanes. They had sweltered when hot winds blew from arid coasts or the off-shore breezes brought the heavy breath of the jungle, stagnant with decay. Other nights they had rocked at anchor in the lee of tropic isles where the plunder of long-dead buccaneers might yet lie buried in rusting, brass-bound chests.

Randy had talked of these things with Frank on their desert camping trips or when they scudded before a brisk breeze in the little sailboat they had made with their own hands. They had dreamed of the time when high school lay behind them and they could become tuna fishermen. And some day, they both vowed, they'd sail together on the *Ripple*.

What of those plans now? Randy wondered, with a catch at his throat. Weeks had passed since Frank had sailed on his first cruise with his uncle Vittorio Castignoni, in the *Westwind*. At first her course could be followed along the Central American coast by wireless reports, by her ship-to-shore radiophone calls. Then came a mysterious silence, lengthening into days—a warning of disaster. All fishermen were alerted and began a search for the missing clipper. Coast Guard planes did their utmost to find her. But no wreckage, not even a skiff bearing her name, was discovered to explain her disappearance. Like the *Belle Isle*, the tuna boat that had vanished without leaving a trace, her fate seemed likely to remain one of the secrets of the sea. Only Randy still refused to abandon hope.

Lost in thought, he failed to notice a big fisherman stepping from a portside door of the *Ripple*. The man swung over the rail to the dock guard block and approached at a rolling seaman's gait. The boy's unhappy face and brimming eyes caught the fisherman's attention and, recognizing Randy, he strode over to grip his arm.

Randy glanced up with a start. There was nothing handsome in the man's broad, red Scandivanian face, with its patchwork of freckles and a nose flattened in some past accident, but there was unmistakable sympathy in the blue eyes. Randy could never remember whether the fellow's name was Hanson or Nelson or something quite different; because his first fishing experience had been on the Great Lakes, everyone called him "Freshwater."

"Missing that pal of yours?" Freshwater asked, his deep voice surprisingly gentle.

Randy swallowed. "I miss Frank like everything!"

· 4 ·

"I'll bet you do! You two were closer than Frank and his brother Louie."

"If it weren't for Louie, Frank would be safe on the *Ripple* right now!"

Freshwater's light brows shot up. "What makes you think so?"

"The only reason Frank made his first trip with his uncle was to learn how to fish before he sailed with his dad. Then Louie wouldn't have the chance to ride him so much."

"So Louie played the big brother with Frank, did he?"

"With both of us," Randy declared heatedly. "Just because he was two years older was no reason why he had to act so superior. Louie's no superman! He never made a single team in high school, and he wasn't so hot in his studies, either. Took him a year longer to finish than it did us!"

"I'll never forget the time the skipper took me to watch your basketball team play another high school," Freshwater recalled. "Most of the players were only fair, but you and Frank always seemed to sense what the other was going to do."

"We'd practised in Frank's backyard from the time we were old enough to shoot a basket," Randy explained, and added, "We'll be teammates again, Freshwater!"

Sympathy showed in the big man's red and homely face. "Don't count too much on that, Randy. The *Westwind's* been missing five weeks."

"Six weeks this evening, Freshwater," the boy said.

The date was fixed firmly in his mind, for that was the night his mother had awakened him from a sound sleep, say-

ing, "The marine operator is calling you, Randy. Hurry—
here's your dressing gown."

As he slipped on the robe, he had asked sleepily, "It must
be Dad. Sure he doesn't want you, Mom?"

"No," said his mother, a little puzzled. "The girl asked
for you."

Half a minute later Randy was at the phone, and the
operator was saying, "Randy Draper? Just a moment. The
Westwind is calling you."

Randy was electrified then to hear an eager and excited
voice that he recognized as Frank Castignoni's. "Well,
sleepy-head, can't you even stay up till nine?"

Randy had glanced quickly at the grandfather clock in the
hall, and then he had grinned. A mental image of Frank's
sparkling black eyes and the flash of his white teeth against
the warm olive of his face had risen before him.

"You tramp, it's midnight! Where are you?"

"Off Panama. I was afraid you'd be away with your
father."

"I haven't had a chance to go fishing yet. Dad's still down
at Cedros Island. Mom heard from him yesterday."

"I thought there'd be less interference on the marine
radiophone if I called you late, Randy," Frank dashed on.
"And I wanted to talk to you before you sailed on your father's eighty-footer. How'd you like to start fishing on a
clipper instead?"

"The *Westwind?*" Randy had demanded eagerly.

"No, no—the *Ripple*."

"Hold everything! If you think I'm going out for the first

time with that big brother of yours. . . ."

"I'll be with you," Frank interrupted. "I'm becoming quite a fisherman, only the others don't suspect it yet. If we're together on Papa's boat, I'll show you the ropes. Even if Louie does throw his weight around, the two of us can handle him. How about it?"

"You're not making me mad," Randy had said with a broad smile. "But will your dad take me?"

"Uncle Vittorio was talking to him just now on the radio-phone, and Papa says Earnesto Antonio wants to retire. I think Papa might take you in his place."

"Try to fix it up, will you, Frank?"

"Sure. Leave it to me." And Frank laughed. "What a team we'll make taking two-pole tuna!"

But since that night, no other word had been heard from the clipper *Westwind*. She had sent out no distress call. And that in itself hinted at catastrophe. An explosion might have destroyed her before Vittorio Castignoni could send out an SOS. . . .

Randy had considered this possibility for weeks, and now, looking at Freshwater, he said doggedly, "I'm going to learn what happened to the *Westwind*. And when I do, maybe I'll find Frank alive."

"You're a stubborn kid!"

Randy had been called that before—by classmates who failed to understand him. The truth was that he was rarely swayed by emotion, seldom acted on impulse as stubborn people did. His decisions on serious problems were likely to be reached only after considerable thought. But then he was as hard to change as a bird dog on a fresh scent—unless someone could convince him he was wrong.

"I don't believe any wooden boat, even the *Belle Isle*, could disappear without leaving a hatch cover, a skiff or some kind of wreckage, Freshwater," Randy said slowly. "Since nothing of that sort has been found, isn't it a hopeful sign?"

The big fisherman did not appear convinced, but he slapped the boy's arm with fellow feeling. "Here's hoping you're right, Randy." And he started on, his rolling gait suggesting that he was still at sea.

Randy watched him disappear into the plant. And then, goading himself for whatever might lie ahead, he clambered aboard the *Ripple*. Somewhere below a hose was hissing, and he walked to the end rail to look down into an opened fish well on the lower deck. He recognized the two fishermen hosing and scrubbing the pipes lining the square walls of the well.

The giant directing the stream of water was Nicco Puccinelli. Helping him with a long-handled brush was Julio Ortorio. They made a strange pair. Puccinelli's powerful chest was bare, and beneath his red crash-helmet his face was given the expression of a startled child's, by wide, dark eyes. Ortorio, who failed to reach his companion's shoulder, wore a battered old felt hat and had the dignified air of a judge. A white mustache, spanning his broad, brown face almost from ear to ear, was apparently intended to hide the white scar on his right cheek. Despite their differences, the two men were drawn together through having come from the same small Italian fishing village. One was seldom seen without the other.

"Is the skipper aboard?" Randy shouted.

Puccinelli turned and the torrent of water from the hose caught the smaller man, hurling him against the pipes of the bulkhead. The giant looked up unaware that Ortorio, now dripping and bristling with indignation, was reaching for the brush he had dropped.

"Who do you want?" bellowed Puccinelli.

"Captain Castignoni," Randy called down. And then, noticing that Ortorio was raising the long-handled brush, he yelled in warning, *"Look out, Puccinelli!"*

Before the man could move, the heavy brush crashed onto the helmet, driving it over Puccinelli's ears. His knees buckled, and he sat down hard.

"You find Joe in his room, Randy," he roared. And then, as if just realizing what had happened, he glanced up with the expression of an injured child. "Why did you do that, Ortorio?"

Ortorio started to speak, then gasped as the hose, thrashing like an angry snake, turned to drench him once more. Puccinelli bellowed when it next sprayed him. Both men were trying to capture the twisting hose when Randy, with a faint grin, turned away.

He walked along the port side, climbed a ladder to the curving bridge surrounding the wheelhouse, and stepped inside. The place was deserted. After a glance at the gyro-compass and steering device mounted between the wheel and the center window, he crossed the house to knock on the captain's door.

Seconds passed before a heavy voice said, "Come in."

Randy opened the door and saw Captain Castignoni sitting on his bunk, facing the chart table. He was a stocky man with iron-gray hair and mustache. His forceful face, burned to a deep bronze by tropical sunlight, was dominated by a hawklike nose and a square jaw. An air of suppressed excitement usually revealed itself in the captain's sparkling black eyes, in his animated expression, his eager gestures and hearty voice. Now Randy was shocked by a feeling that the warm and vital spirit had gone out of Castignoni.

Making a listless motion toward the desk chair, he said, "Sit down, Randy. I suppose you came to inquire about Frank."

Dropping into the chair, Randy nodded.

The captain stared with somber dark eyes at the rows of shallow drawers beneath the chart table for several moments.

"We've learned nothing more about the *Westwind*," he declared, as if speaking were an effort. "These things happen. Tuna boats are hard to trim in heavy seas because they carry so much weight aft. Oil and water get in motion, swishing in wells and tanks, making them unstable. They can turn turtle in a twinkling. Other things destroy our boats, too. If a spark reaches oil floating in the bilge, there's an explosion. Or a boat may run aground and be beaten to wreckage by tremendous ground swells. You're a fisherman's son, Randy. You know how these things go. We lose an average of one boat in ten every year. It was Frank's bad luck to be on that lost boat."

The low, carefully controlled voice was so unlike the captain's old boisterous, excited manner of speaking that Randy had a feeling he was listening to a stranger. And Captain Castignoni was certainly not that! He had been a family friend and a neighbor for many years.

"But there are usually survivors," Randy suggested anxiously. "If Frank and others got ashore in a boat, somewhere in the jungle . . ."

"In that case," interrupted Castignoni, "they'd be passed along from one native village to another as in the past. Or an Indian runner would bring out a message to the nearest telegraph or radio station." He pointed to a calendar, with days crossed out by heavy pencil strokes. "I've counted the days, then the weeks—hoping something like that would take place. But too much time has gone by for that to happen now."

"The *Westwind* was off the Panama coast when Frank called me," Randy said. "The papers didn't report any storm at the time."

"Not then, no. But later, when the *Westwind* was presumably sailing northward, there were *Chubascos, Tehuantepecers,* and *Papagayos* off the Central American coast. All local names for hurricanes, Randy!"

Randy's eyes brimmed. Had the clipper Frank was on capsized in a tropical storm? Had the weight of tuna in her wells made her break amidships under the impacts of wind and sea? *But why had no wreckage been found?*

Captain Castignoni began tapping the bunkboard as if impatient to end their talk. Randy suddenly realized that he

· 11 ·

had failed to speak of the matter that had brought him.

"There's a mystery about the *Westwind*," he went on rapidly. "Where there's a mystery, there must be some sort of clues—if anyone will look for them. I want to find them, sir. . . ." His voice broke, and it was a moment before he could gasp anxiously, "Could I sail with you, sir?"

The captain regarded him with a puzzled frown. "Why don't you sign on your father's boat?"

"She's too small."

"*Too small!* You can learn to fish as well on her as on a clipper!"

"Yes, Captain," Randy went on hurriedly, "but Dad doesn't carry enough Diesel oil to sail much south of Cedros Island."

"True enough, but . . ." Castignoni's gray brows arched. "What of it?"

"If the *Westwind* disappeared on her way north, any clues must be south of Cedros. She wouldn't have sailed that far from Panama without reporting to the cannery how many tons of fish she was bringing in and when she'd arrive."

"The *Westwind*, the *Westwind!*" Captain Castignoni exploded, as if his patience were sorely tried.

Springing up, he strode into the wheelhouse, flinging over his shoulder an angry torrent of words: "You crazy kid, do you think I don't miss my own son, my brother? Do you think I haven't searched constantly this last trip for any clues to their disappearance?"

Shaken by the outburst, Randy sat motionless, feeling a cold numbness creeping over him. He'd sure made a mess of it! If Captain Castignoni wouldn't take him southward, who would? Then his dogged determination reasserted itself. He wouldn't give up that easily! He'd find some skipper who would sign him on, even though he had no experience as a fisherman!

But it was nevertheless with a sick feeling of defeat that Randy rose and walked slowly into the wheelhouse. Castignoni stared from the window across the narrowed bay, where sun motes danced on the water and a Navy launch was skimming by.

"I'm sorry, Captain," Randy murmured, turning toward the door.

"Wait," said the skipper; and when Randy swung around he saw that the angry flush had faded from Castignoni's face. "I guess we're both pretty cut up about Frank, aren't we?"

"Yes, sir. He was . . ." Randy's voice trailed off and he spread his hands helplessly, at a loss for words. "Being with him was always fun because—well, we enjoyed the same things. We were so much alike in so many ways."

The captain started. "So much alike," he repeated slowly. His black eyes studied the boy in an intent appraisal. An abrupt change then came over the man. Rapidly he began striding across the wheelhouse, waving his arms. Once more he was the Captain Castignoni that Randy regarded almost as a second father: his dark face was animated, his eyes glowed. "Of course! Of course!" he shouted, as if making some remarkable discovery. "I must be blind!"

Randy stared in amazement, wondering what had brought about this startling reaction.

Suddenly the captain ceased his excited pacing and pointed a stocky finger at the boy. "Don't expect me to be easy on you because you're the son of my friend Bob Draper."

A tingle darted down Randy's spine. "You mean I can sail on the *Ripple,* sir?" he cried hoarsely.

"I've laid down the conditions!"

"I understand." And Randy flushed. "I won't expect favors, Captain. I'll do my share."

"No, no!" cried the captain in a quick, excited voice. "From Louie, from Freshwater, from Ortorio and Puccinelli and the others, that would be sufficient. But from you I'll expect more!"

"I—I'm not sure that I do understand," faltered Randy.

"Then I will make it clear." The captain's eyes had a penetrating quality and his dark face had become stern. "From you I'll demand what I would of Frank. Your share will not be enough! *You will do what I tell you!*"

Eagerly Randy agreed. "Anything, sir."

"Good!" muttered the captain, his eyes becoming pensive. "Antonio was Louie's partner on two-pole tuna. You will take his place. . . ."

The skipper's next words fell on deaf ears. Randy was thinking of the abuse that he and Frank had taken from Louie. The blood seemed to be drumming painfully in his head. Fish with Louie? Never! But when he was on the verge of protest, he remembered the captain's conditions: *You will do what I tell you.* Well, to find Frank he could even endure Louie's sharp tongue, though it wouldn't be pleasant.

· 14 ·

The captain halted abruptly, his eyes widening. "Ah, but I forgot! At seventeen you'll need your father's permission! And he won't be back in time. We sail tonight."

"I'm sure my mother will let me go," Randy put in quickly.

Castignoni snapped his fingers. "Yes, yes—my wife could not decide this, but your mother will."

And Randy understood what the captain meant. Mrs. Castignoni was a plump, merry little woman, an able house-keeper and a good cook, but deciding whether her son could go to sea would be beyond her. She had relied on Frank to make such decisions from the time he was ten. It was Frank who turned the shut-off valve and called the plumber when a water-pipe burst. It was he who paid the bills, sent the car to be repaired, or bargained for the upholstering of the davenport with broken springs. It had seemed odd to Randy that Mrs. Castignoni could not manage such problems as his mother did, and even stranger that Frank rather than his older brother would take charge during his father's absences at sea. But once, when he had asked Frank about it, his friend had looked bewildered. "Why, I never thought about it, Randy. I guess it just happened that way in our family."

"If your mother says it's all right," Castignoni now concluded, "go buy your gear, Randy. We'll sail from Fishermen's Wharf at midnight."

It was eleven that night when Randy stopped the car at Fishermen's Wharf. For a moment he sat, hands idle on the wheel, before turning to grin at his mother, seated beside him.

"Take care of yourself, Mom," he said. "You're on your own now."

His mother smiled back. She was a tall woman, with soft brown hair parted mid-center above an oval face. Though not pretty in the ordinary sense, her vivacious expression and the serene humor in her gray eyes gave her a warmth that Randy always found appealing.

"I'll manage," his mother said. "Write if you have the chance, Randy."

"Better than that," he promised, opening the door, "I'll call ship-to-shore some night if I catch enough fish to pay the charges."

Hurrying around the car, he lifted his heavy sea-bag from the back seat and dropped it on the sidewalk. He hesitated then, for he knew the period ahead would be a lonely one for his mother and he wished to say something to make it easier. Maybe by telling her how much the trust and understanding in their family had meant to him. But the right words would not come.

In the end, he made a helpless, uncertain gesture and blurted, "Everything's always been swell in our home, Mom. You—and Dad—and the way we feel about each other— and . . ." He broke off abruptly, laughing. "I'm making an awful bobble of this."

"Not so awful." And he saw his mother's eyes glistening.

"What I mean," he said, picking up his bag, "is to take this like a man, Mom."

He didn't realize his blunder until his mother's laughter rang out in a sudden musical peal as she slid over to take her place at the steering wheel. He turned, grinned sheepishly and waved before plodding on through the knots of fishermen and Navy seamen on the wharf.

Farther along the harbor lights showed him the gleaming white bulk of a tuna clipper. When he reached her, he made sure she was the *Ripple,* and then cast his bag aboard. No one was on deck as he climbed over the rail, but a globe blazed at the masthead and light shone from several of the main-deck portholes.

Randy swung the bag over a shoulder and strode along deck to what he knew was the galley door. Stepping inside, he saw seven fishermen at a table in the opposite corner. Before them was a large platter of meat and cheese, a loaf of bread, a number of heavy mugs and a giant coffee-pot. Their faces lighted and there was a chorus of shouts.

"Toss him overboard!"

"Put him in the bait-tank."

"Let's set him to swabbing the decks."

"Silence, silence!" shouted Julio Ortorio reprovingly. "This is no proper way to greet a new mate!" Squeezing closer to Puccinelli, he patted the bench beside him. "Sit down, my friend, and ignore these rough fellows."

"Thanks, Ortorio," Randy said with a grin. "But I've got to sign on. Where can I stow my gear?"

"Take Antonio's bunk," suggested Freshwater.

"He's too late," said a curt voice. "I've already moved down from my upper bunk to Antonio's. Randy can take mine; he'll enjoy being hurled out whenever we're in heavy seas."

The unfriendly speaker was Louie Castignoni. He was as large as Randy, and even heavier. He might have been handsome save for his somber expression and sullen mouth. On his left wrist he wore a heavy silver band—a man's bracelet, intricately wrought by a Navajo silversmith and set with several bluish-green matrices of turquoise. It had surprised Frank and Randy the day Louie had bought it with his first pay check. Since that time he was never seen without the silver wristband.

Louie swallowed his coffee and, with a show of annoyance, pushed back his chair. "Come on, I'll tuck you in."

Randy followed the hulking youth out of the galley and to the cabin door, which Louie swung out and latched. When he had switched on the light, Randy saw three pair of bunks on either side. Beyond them were lockers and a washroom.

"Nice cabin," he commented, pleased by its cleanliness and the hardwood paneling of bunkboards and lockers.

"We call it *room*," Louie brusquely corrected him. He put his hand on the bare mattress of an upper bunk and said, "This is yours." Then pointing to a locker with a neatly-lettered *A*, he added, "That was Antonio's—yours now. And in the big cupboard above it you'll find the linen to make up your sack."

"Thanks, Louie. Your dad says I'll be your teammate."

"It's tough all over," Louie said dryly. "See that you pull your weight when we're fishing together, or you'll hear from me!"

· 18 ·

With that ungracious threat, Louie lumbered out.

Randy squeezed the sea-bag into his locker and hurried up to the bridge. By the blue glare of a light over the gyrocompass, he found the captain in conversation with a compactly built man of medium height, whose visored cap was tilted back at a jaunty angle, exposing a lock of fair hair. The weird illumination emphasized the man's square chin and the humorous squint of his ice-blue eyes.

Breaking off the conversation, the captain asked, "Your mother gave her permission, Randy?"

"Yes, sir."

"Meet Steve Vardon, our navigator and the pilot of our plane."

"Steve to my friends, Randy," said Vardon, firmly gripping the boy's hand. Though Randy liked the navigator's friendly manner, he sensed a headstrong, untamed quality in Steve Vardon.

"I think Frank mentioned you," said Randy. "But that was months ago."

Steve laughed. "I was probably on the *Westwind* then."

Steve had served on the missing clipper! But before Randy could ask about her, the captain called him into the office to sign on the boat's articles. When this detail was attended to, they returned to the wheelhouse and the skipper headed toward the portside door.

"I'll go below for a cup of coffee, Steve. The Chief should have the fuel pump working in a few minutes. Then we'll shove off."

"Captain," Randy said, as Castignoni reached the door,

"am I assigned to the port or starboard watch?"

Castignoni turned, and the blue compass light showed that his strong face was set in rigid lines.

"A captain stands no watch," he said sternly. "I'm responsible for the safety of my vessel at all times. Were Frank serving under me, I'd demand as much from him. He'd be on call day or night, regardless of watches, whenever or wherever he was needed." Allowing a brief pause for his words to sink in, the captain added gruffly, *"And that's what I'm expecting of you!"*

Taken aback by the sharp tone, it was several moments before Randy could murmur faintly, "Yes, sir."

"Then we understand each other," snapped the captain, swinging on his heel.

As his footsteps died away on the ladder, Steve whistled softly. "Block-buster!" he said. "What did you do to ruffle up the skipper?"

"I—honestly, I don't know, Steve."

"Joe has changed a lot since he lost his youngest son and his brother on the *Westwind*," observed Steve. "But I've never heard him talk to anyone quite like that. The fisherman who is unpopular with his captain has a mighty rough time of it, Randy. In your shoes, I'd make an all-time record getting my gear ashore."

Randy suspected that Steve would do just that. For the navigator looked like a man who would buckle under to no one.

But if he took his gear ashore, he'd not only lose his chance to become a fisherman on one of the larger tuna boats, but his chance to solve the mystery of the *Westwind's* disappearance would also be gone. Randy had promised himself that he would clear up that mystery if any clues still existed.

"Louie will be a thorny problem, Steve, and it looks as if Captain Castignoni has it in for me, too," Randy said doggedly. "But I can take it! I've got to stick it out to find Frank!"

A slow smile lighted the navigator's face and he put out a hand to squeeze the boy's shoulder. "Sorry, kid."

"What for?" Randy asked in surprise.

"For underestimating you."

A warm surge of gratitude swept through Randy. He foresaw plenty of difficulties in the days ahead, but they'd be easier to bear now. He knew he could count on the friendship of Steve Vardon.

CHAPTER TWO

Randy Learns Seamanship

the Hard Way

A SHORT TIME after the captain had gone to his room, there appeared on the bridge a stocky little man with a fringe of hair encircling his round, bald head. He was Anthony Riggio, one of the two fishermen who assisted the engineer. He nodded at Steve, smiled warmly at Randy and went to knock on the captain's door.

"The Chief says everything's under control, Joe," he shouted.

Castignoni stepped out. "All aboard, Riggio?"

"Every last man. I checked coming up."

With a nod the skipper walked to the portside and pulled a cord. A bell clanged. Footsteps began to pound along the deck. The boy turned toward the door, planning to help cast off the lines. A gruff command from the captain stopped him.

"Stay here, Randy. You might learn something."

Joe Castignoni shoved the lever of the engine-room telegraph, a large brass instrument mounted near the wheel. Randy heard a low humming. The boat vibrated with the pulse of her Diesel engines; there was a gushing sound of the screw churning up water astern.

From below a voice bellowed, "All clear, Joe."

Steve Vardon pulled the bell cord. The captain levered the telegraph once more and stepped onto the duckboards before the wheel. As they began moving, women's voices penetrated the deep throbbing of the engines. Randy stepped to the portside window and saw fishermen's wives waving as water opened between boat and wharf.

"Stand here and watch what I'm doing," the captain said sharply.

Randy hastened to obey. The captain spun the wheel, and as the stern swung the boat shook with the thrust of her propeller. The *Ripple* chugged past a south-bound swordfishing boat, with a long harpooner's plank extending from her bow, then by a Navy destroyer. The lights of wharves and piers, of the city to the eastward began to drop astern, leaving only silvery streaks on water that gleamed like black marble. Randy watched a plane leaving Lindbergh Field, and moments later it was buzzing over the boat, its wing lights tracing darting lines of color across the gray overcast.

The clipper was no longer chugging now. Smoothly she glided, the calm water whispering along her hull. Randy was startled by a dark and looming shape off to port. Looking up, he saw the jutting deck of an aircraft carrier sliding by. Before long the *Ripple* slipped along the channel between North Island and the sheltering shoulder of land to the north, past Ballast Point and the bluffs of Point Loma. And then, rolling gently in the ocean swells, she turned southward.

Randy and his friend Frank had often ventured into the open Pacific in their small sailboat. But this was different.

· 23 ·

He felt a stir of excitement as he realized the great adventure was beginning. For many weeks the *Ripple* would cruise sunny seas in pursuit of the ever-wandering schools of tuna before returning to her home port. Would he find any trace of the *Westwind* in these weeks ahead?

It was nearly two in the morning when South Coronado Island dropped astern. Then it was dark off to port except for the infrequent lights of late cars speeding along the narrow causeway of the Silver Strand. Randy's eyes were growing heavy and he hoped the skipper would soon suggest that he leave the bridge.

Castignoni swung from the wheel now and set his course on the automatic pilot. As the device took control, the wheel began to make short jerks, first one way, then the other. The captain yawned and stretched his arms. "Rout me out at eight bells, Steve," he said.

"Two men aren't needed on graveyard watch, Joe," observed Steve.

Castignoni appeared to bristle. "You're a good navigator," he said curtly. "Suppose you stick to that, Steve, and leave the boy to me."

The navigator's jaw stiffened. "I like the kid," he said evenly. "And I like you, Joe. But if you think I'm going to stand by while . . ."

Randy sensed that Steve was fighting mad, though the only clue to his anger was the slight narrowing of his ice-blue eyes.

"That's all right, Steve," the boy hastily broke in. "I made an agreement with the captain, and I want to keep it."

Castignoni's face had been growing cold, but now he peered at the boy in surprise. Then, with a shrug, he stalked to his cabin and slammed the door.

The navigator walked to the window. Randy went to another window, for there was nothing for them to do but watch for vessels on their course. The automatic pilot was steering the boat through the darkness.

"Where did you learn to fly, Steve?" Randy asked after a long silence.

"I enlisted in the Air Force. Before I finished training, the Allies had the Normandy landing well behind them. Two months after I got into action Germany surrendered. I was transferred to the Pacific for the wind-up against the Japs."

"What did you do after getting your discharge, Steve?"

"I was a bush pilot in Alaska for a while, then for a year I was hopping the Andes in some surplus crates a Chilean operator was trying to build into an airline. When he could buy better planes, it was like driving a taxi. So I went to the South Pacific to fly ore out of a New Guinea gold mine in a converted bomber. One day they overloaded that baby and she conked out. After walking away from the wreckage and getting a fine case of malaria making my way out through the jungle, I decided to see what it was like at home."

"That's when you became Vittorio Castignoni's navigator?"

"Not right away. I held some other jobs before I took a navigation course and got my papers in order to replace his navigator, who had bought his own boat."

"How long did you sail on the *Westwind?*" Randy asked.

"Only one cruise. By then I was growing restless for a plane. Joe Castignoni had bought a small hydroplane to scout for tuna, so I became his pilot and navigator."

Randy was going to question Steve about the *Westwind* when his friend changed the subject.

"Joe is acting mighty strange for a man once known as an easy skipper. Are you sure you haven't stirred him up in some way, Randy?"

"Not in any way I can think of," Randy said. And he described, as well as he could remember, the captain's behavior during their conversation before the *Ripple* had sailed.

"Waved his arms, eh?" muttered Steve. "Said, 'I must be blind!'? What could he mean? I don't get it."

Randy was almost asleep on his feet when the bell clanged eight times to end the graveyard watch at four in the morning. Moments later "Doc" Bernedetto, a member of the port watch, reached the bridge. He was a large man, wearing plain gold-rimmed glasses, and in better clothing he might easily have passed for a successful professional man.

"Hi, Doc," Randy said.

Bernedetto beamed, for he liked the nickname.

Captain Castignoni opened his door and, with a stern glance at Randy, said, "Get some rest. I want you back here when we enter our first Mexican port in a few hours."

His words seemed to confirm Steve's suspicion that the skipper was bearing down unreasonably on his new crew member. But Randy was too tired to think about that now. He stumbled down to his room, wearily made up his bunk and turned in. It seemed as if his head had scarcely touched the pillow before Louie was roughly shaking him awake.

"Pile out, if you want your breakfast."

The salty breeze, blowing through the open porthole, helped clear Randy's head as he washed and dressed.

He stepped out into the brilliant sunlight. For a moment he paused, watching the *Ripple* pitching gently as she sliced through the long, glistening swells.

Then he entered the galley. George Terraza was at the stove, frying big slices of ham and hotcakes. He was a plump man, with a face as round as a pumpkin, and a crisp white chef's hat adorned his head. The headgear had reposed there every time Randy had seen the cook. It was always so clean and heavily starched that the boy had wondered whether Terraza had a fresh hat for every hour of the day.

"The skipper says not to serve you," remarked the cook. "He wants you topside right away."

Randy looked at the men eating their breakfast. Louie favored him with a sardonic grin. Then, with a flush of anger he wheeled and left the galley.

He found the captain at the wheel, staring southward. But whether he was peering at the jagged, rocky Mexican coast or at the distant mountains, looming bare and brown against the deep blue sky, Randy could not tell.

"You'll eat with me later," said the skipper, without turning.

Though it seemed a strange demand, the anger died in Randy. At least he wasn't to be deprived of breakfast!

Minutes later the captain turned eastward and the clipper

passed into Ensenada Bay. Lazy rollers, glistening silver in the morning sunlight, broke in creaming surges along the crescent shoreline. To the southward Randy saw the shark-processing plant, facing on the white-sand beach where he and Frank had once camped. It was not there, however, but toward a recess at the head of the bay that the *Ripple* was proceeding. Warehouses, small hotels and homes looked down upon this recess, and on the northwest side two piers reached out from the shore.

When the boat was within half a mile of the least rickety of the piers, the captain pushed the telegraph lever, and the rumble of the engines faded away. As the clipper drifted to a stop, Castignoni pulled a cord to blow a blast with the boat's whistle.

Once more the crew demonstrated its efficiency. It surprised Randy that the fishermen could go about their duties in the cheerfully informal way of men on a holiday outing, and yet do their work so well. The boy's ears had not ceased ringing from the shrill whistling, when Puccinelli and Ortorio appeared at the forward capstan. Though they bickered as they let go the anchor, it soon splashed overboard, chain rattling and clanking until the hook reached bottom. And at that moment the mastman strode through the wheelhouse to the captain's room, reappearing shortly with two flags. Jack Lucca was tall and slender, with a hint of shyness in his manner, and his face had an unmistakable friendliness when lighted by his boyish smile.

"Give Lucca a hand, Randy," the captain said gruffly.

Randy descended the ladder behind the mastman and followed him along deck to the pole. Lucca hauled down the flag line and snapped on the two pieces of bunting. One bore the Mexican eagle, with a writhing rattlesnake in its beak, on a green, white-and-red background, while the other was the plain yellow quarantine flag used in entering foreign ports. Lucca pulled them up to the masthead, where they whipped lightly in the soft breeze.

"Simple, isn't it, Randy?" he asked, with a trace of self-consciousness.

Ten minutes later a pilot boat put out from the larger pier, rising and falling as it cut through the swells. When it drew into the lee, or protected side of the *Ripple,* a Jacob's ladder was secured and three Mexican officers used it to clamber aboard. Two were round and short and had the coppery faces of Indians, but the third was taller and had brown hair as curly as Randy's. Castignoni addressed him as Obregon, making Randy suspect that the man had had an Irish ancestor named O'Brien.

"Breakfast is awaiting us," the skipper announced heartily.

"*No, no, Capitán,*" protested Obregon. "We have eaten."

"None of that, *amigos.*" Castignoni laughed and with a nod at Randy to follow them, he slipped an arm around the tall Mexican and headed toward the galley.

After they were seated, the captain introduced Randy, and then appeared to forget him. Gaily the men talked and laughed as they ate. The officers attempted to speak English. Castignoni replied in their tongue. Randy had studied enough Spanish in high school to know that the Mexicans were having the better of the exchange. As he ate in silence and listened to the spirited conversation, he wondered why he had been included in the party.

At length Terraza cleared the table. Castignoni sent Randy for a portfolio on his desk, and when the boy returned with it he removed a sheaf of papers and spread them before the officers.

Obregon examined each sheet briefly before passing it along to the other Mexicans. *"Si, si, Capitán,"* he said. "Clearance papers, bait-seining permit, fishing permit, licenses for your men . . ." He was counting the latter when suddenly his brows lifted. "Am I wrong? Eleven licenses and twelve men?"

Castignoni's black eyes rolled upward, and he clapped his forehead. *"Estupido!"* he groaned. "I forgot to tell Randy here. . . ."

"I—I'm the one who forgot," faltered Randy. And drawing a wallet from his pocket, he laid a form before the tall Mexican officer. "I got this after you said I could sail with you."

Obregon's white teeth flashed. "All is in order." He laid a friendly hand on Randy's shoulder and asked, "Your son, *Capitán?"*

The skipper gave Randy a long, searching glance and then laughed. "Not quite, *mi amigo.* Not quite."

Though the statement appeared to be another sign of puzzling behavior on the captain's part, the boy felt relieved. Castignoni at least showed no annoyance at Randy's failure to deliver the license earlier.

Within five minutes the Mexican officials had filled out the necessary forms and left the clipper. They waved and shouted, *"Gracias, Capitán,"* as the pilot boat sped away.

The skipper waved back until the officers entered the cabin, and then he curtly ordered Randy to follow him to the bridge. He left the boy in the wheelhouse, going into his room to look at the chart. The boat trembled as the anchor chain, rasping and clanking, was heaved up. Presently the navigator appeared, and walked into the captain's quarters.

"I wonder if we might pick up bait at Guadalupe Island, Steve."

"It's a hundred miles out of our way, Joe."

"Be worth that—if we run onto a school of tuna before we reach Magdalena Bay." After a moment the captain said, "I'm going to chance it."

He came to take the wheel. Upon completing a wide turn he headed toward the entrance of the bay, and then left the duckboards. "Take her out to deep water, Randy."

The boy's knees suddenly shook, his mouth became dry and his eyes darted toward the captain in alarm. Clearly Castignoni was not joking!

He's trying to scare me, thought Randy. *And he's sure doing it, too! But maybe if I take the helm, he'll see what a crazy thing it is to have a beginner at the wheel in a place like this.*

His legs seemed almost too weak to support him when he stepped onto the duckboards. The bay entrance was so wide that Randy would not have given it a second thought had he been at the tiller of his sailboat. But that was quite different from being at the helm of a hundred-foot clipper. His palms were damp as he gripped the spokes of the wheel, turning too far starboard, then too far to port. That the clipper must be leaving a zigzag wake was only too plain, but Randy could not steer a straight course, try as he would.

The captain did not relieve him, however. Instead, he groaned and said, "This is too painful to watch." And striding into his room, he slammed the door.

Steve grinned. "Relax, Randy. Let the wheel click a few times—that's enough. Spin hard over only for wide turns. And watch the gyro-compass needle."

Randy tried no more spectacular turns of the wheel. Nevertheless, he continued to turn too far, so that he had to keep correcting his mistakes. Nor could he keep the binnacle needle from dancing first one way, then the other.

"Everyone puts too much beef into it when they're learning," declared Steve. "Now watch."

Standing beside Randy, he spun the wheel a little port, a little starboard. The vessel responded smoothly. The example helped, but Randy still steered a somewhat wavering course out through the entrance. The *Ripple* bounded lightly in the glassy swells, and for minutes Steve made no comment.

"We're far enough off the coast now," he decided at length. "Let's see if I can remember our position so that I can set our course for Guadalupe Island."

When the automatic pilot was locked, the wheel began to jerk as if gripped with an invisible hand. Randy stepped from the duckboards with a sigh of relief.

The navigator's pale-blue eyes crinkled. "Lived through it,

eh? I'd suggest you snatch a little sleep before the Old Man thinks up another job for you, Randy. Apparently he's determined to make you regret you ever signed on this packet!"

Randy had no chance to make up lost sleep, however, for he met Louie leaving their room.

"Now that your big-shot Mexican pals have left," said Louie sarcastically, "suppose you start working on your fishing gear."

"Can't I use Antonio's poles?" asked Randy.

"He was smaller than you. You'll need ten-foot bamboos."

Reluctantly Randy followed Louie. Under the overhang of the main deck, men had spread mats on the hatch-covers. Some dozed, while others worked on their fishing gear—replacing lines, piano-wire leaders, or the feathered jigs. Trailed through the water, these lures resembled squids, the tuna's favorite food, and they were known by that name.

From a rack under the bait-tank canopy, Louie selected eight poles of Japanese bamboo—the only type sufficiently strong for tuna fishing—and cut them down to proper size. Then he set Randy to sanding the joints.

The boy polished with sandpaper until his hands were raw; but each time he stopped, Louie would yell at him, "Smooth, I said! Keep sanding until they're like glass."

It was noon before Randy's poles were polished to suit Louie's critical taste. And he spent the remainder of the day rigging them with lines and leaders. He needed only a single four-foot line, a wire leader and a feathered squid for fish weighing up to thirty-five pounds. Few men could take aboard heavier fish in any quantity without help, however, so a more complicated arrangement was required for larger tuna.

When Randy fished with Louie each would use his own pole and their lines would be connected by a swivel to a single leader to take what were known as "two-pole tuna." Another rig had to be prepared for yellowfins of seventy to a hundred pounds, for then Freshwater's pole and line would also be made fast to their swivel. Steve Vardon or the captain would join their team with still another bamboo and leader when they were taking four-polers weighing up to a hundred and fifty pounds. And besides this gear with squids, another set had to be rigged up. It was identical to the first, save for the bare hook, to be used when tuna refused the feathered lures and bait was required.

The unfamiliar work would have been hard enough for Randy without Louie's constant stream of biting comments. But when the hulking young man lumbered off to wash up for supper, Freshwater came over to look at the poles and nodded his approval. "Louie's fussy," he said. "But no one makes better gear than he does."

"Maybe not," said Randy. "But I'm sure glad I'm through."

"By switching jigs you'll have a spare set of poles, but you'll need others in case some break, Randy. You'll spend all your spare time working on your gear as long as you're fishing."

After breakfast the following morning Randy went up to the bridge. Steve Vardon stood looking from an open win-

· 34 ·

dow, for the boat was still on automatic pilot. His officer's cap was pushed back, and the breeze ruffled his blond hair.

"Whopper, isn't she?" he demanded, and for the first time Randy noticed the high, mountainous island rising from the sea. "Guadalupe's twenty miles long and about seven wide. And the summit at this end is 4,500 feet."

The soaring slopes gave Randy a feeling of excitement. It was the first time he had been close to one of the desert islands of the Mexican coast. Still perhaps ten miles distant, its black, volcanic cliffs soared in dramatic fashion from the water. A suggestion of forest covered the upper reaches, though Randy could not see the trees clearly because of hovering clouds. C424559 CO. SCHOOLS

The captain appeared at that moment. "Lucca's going up to the barrel," he said, and pointed to binoculars hanging against the bulkhead. "Better take that glass, Randy, and go with him."

Randy felt as though he had eaten too much breakfast. Heights always bothered him. But he had promised to obey the captain, and it was not in his nature to go back on his word if he could avoid it. Now he was beginning to understand, however, what his agreement would mean.

"Yes, s-sir," he said, taking the case.

The rangy mastman was already starting up the rope rigging. Seeing Randy, he paused to ask, "Want to climb up to the crow's nest?"

"No," Randy answered with a scared smile, "but I'm coming!"

Grasping a rope, he swung onto the rail. Uneasily he swallowed at observing the water streaming by the hull. Then he started up the rigging, a rung at a time. The vessel rode steadily, but the higher he ascended the more pronounced became the swaying of the mast from port to starboard with the boat's rolling. He clung to the ropes with knotted hands, knowing that if he lost his grip, he'd fall overboard or be badly injured in striking the deck.

But he did not realize how high he had climbed until he stopped to look down. The clipper seemed to have shrunk in size. Louie, grinning up at him from the lower deck, appeared smaller than Julio Ortorio. His evident enjoyment of Randy's distress was perhaps just what the younger boy needed.

He thinks I've lost my nerve, reflected Randy. *I'll show him!*

Doggedly he dragged himself upward, thoroughly frightened but determined not to back down. Jack Lucca was already in the small, metal enclosure near the top of the mast. He gave Randy a hand. "I got cold feet the first time I tried it," Lucca admitted.

Randy smiled faintly. "I'd balk ten times before I'd do it again!"

The mastman braced himself, for the crow's nest was swinging through wide arcs, the sea drawing nearer, then receding. Removing a small glass from his pocket, he began to scan the approaching island and the sea to either side. Suddenly he uttered a low whistle.

Randy squatted for better balance, took the captain's glass from its case and turned it on the towering black headland at the north end of Guadalupe Island, still several miles away. The powerful lens made it seem quite close. At the summit he made out a sparse forest of pines and palms, of wind-gnarled cypresses and immense, spreading oaks, while below the trees were small white splotches on the slopes, some in motion. "Goats!" he exclaimed.

"Yes," said Lucca. "But bring your glass down. See the big headland—North Point? Well, move to the right of it."

Farther along, on the ocean side of the island, Randy now spied hundreds of birds circling into view and then disappearing into what appeared to be a break in the rock walls.

"The skipper had a good hunch," said Lucca. "Those are cormorants and pelicans. The way they are wheeling makes it pretty certain that they're finding fish in the small cove there. Let's go down. I'll see you don't fall."

The mastman dropped onto the rigging. He directed Randy's feet onto the rungs when the boy, with nervous misgivings, followed him. Randy got a firm grip on the ropes. After that the rest was easy.

Preparations had already begun for taking bait. Doc Bernedetto—known as the "chummer," because he was in charge of the small fish or "chums" used in attracting tuna —was turning a valve on one of the big boxlike structures at the stern. A pump began to rumble, and sea water gushed into one of the bait tanks.

Randy saw other fishermen collecting on the lower deck. He hurried down to join them. Riggio opened the door of a storage room, and the men grasped a net, dragging layer after layer from the room until it lay heaped on deck. Riggio then brought out a battered copper diving helmet, coils of line and air hose, a hand pump and two enormous rubber boots, large enough for even such a giant as Puccinelli.

The captain appeared and studied this gear with a frown. "Why don't you use that aqua-lung and dress I bought you, Riggio? It cost me nearly three hundred dollars."

"I told you why, Joe," Riggio said grimly. "I can slip out of these boots and my helmet and come up, if anything goes wrong. In your gear I might drown!"

"Some day I'll try that aqua-lung myself," the captain muttered irritably. Glancing at the mastman, he said, "Call the Chief, Lucca."

While they waited, Randy returned the binoculars to the wheelhouse. Coming out, he heard sounds overhead, and looked up to see Puccinelli and Ortorio on the cabin, removing a tarpaulin from the motor launch stowed there. He watched them free the lashings holding it, and then descended to the lower deck.

The engineer, William McDowd, was already at the winch below the mast. He was a dour little man, with a grizzled, deeply lined face; and his hoarse grunt, as he started the machine, was almost like a growl.

"Hear that?" marveled Bernedetto with a grin. "Mac's learning to talk."

McDowd whirled about, glaring from beneath his shaggy brows. His tight mouth twitched as though he were about to make a cutting remark. Apparently the effort was too great, however, for the Chief snorted and turned back to the winch. He pushed several levers to lower and spin the boom halfway about, then dropped a big hook dangling from a wire rope, to the pair on the captain's cabin.

The skipper stood well aft, directing the operation. When Puccinelli and Ortorio had slipped a wire over the hook and had made it fast to the speedboat's lifting rings, he called, "Okay, Chief."

McDowd moved the lever to pluck the motor-boat from its chocks. Swinging it around, he lowered it to the well deck as lightly as a feather.

"Better get the other boats ready," decided the captain.

Stowed bottoms up between the rail and the starboard side of the bait tanks, were two smaller craft. The larger of these, the net skiff, was so heavy that the men staggered beneath its weight as they brought it forward. But the smaller skiff, used to support the net, was an easy load for four men. The seine for taking sardines was now piled into the stern of the net skiff, while the diving gear went into the forward end.

Randy glanced off to port and saw that the *Ripple* had passed North Point and was now sailing a quarter-mile to the westward of Guadalupe Island. Sheerwater cliffs rose in sweeping black palisades, patterned here and there by swirls of ancient lava flows. Great bubbles had formed in other places where streams of molten material had been arrested in headlong rush to the sea and had hardened. The ocean had tunneled caverns into the heart of old craters; and above these openings the rock walls were pitted with the small cones of lava vents. Farther southward, talus slopes of shale bulged from the base of the high cliffs.

When the clipper turned toward an opening in the rocky

palisades, the captain went topside to take the wheel, leaving Steve Vardon free to join the men on deck. Slowly the boat glided between the high ramparts and then spread suds astern as she backed and maneuvered into the lee of the western arm of the cove, where boats could safely be launched.

This was quickly accomplished. Steve and Julio Ortorio settled themselves in the speedboat and William McDowd whisked it over the side, holding it poised above the water while Steve started the engine. When the motor was popping and blue clouds of smoke pouring from the exhaust pipe, the Chief lowered the boat. The two men freed the hooks at either end, and it sped away, leaving space for the skiffs to be launched.

Two men were then swung over the side in the net skiff and it was set down. Lines were cast to Riggio and Louie, so that they could pull the boat in close. Randy and three others dropped onto the net and found places on the thwarts. Louie sent a line spinning to Ortorio, who made it fast to a towing bitt. The speedboat slowly began circling, with the net skiff in tow. When it completed its circle, the smaller boat was in the water. A rope soon connected it to the net skiff.

Steve promptly started toward the eastern side of the cove with the two boats skimming astern. Cormorants and pelicans whirled above the tiny armada, their excited cries echoing from the precipitous rock walls. Other birds bobbed on the water until the speedboat was but a few feet from them. Then they would either dive or taxi away in short, skittering flights. The pelicans, with their long beaks and sedate air of dignity, fascinated Randy.

He was watching one of these broad-beaked birds as it stared downward in search of small fish, when he was startled by the appearance of two great animals. They butted and jostled one another as they rose through the clear green water. When they broke the surface Randy saw that they resembled gigantic seals. But they had short, flexible snouts which they raised to roar a deafening challenge.

Randy turned in alarm to Jack Lucca on the thwart beside him. "They're fighting! What are they?"

"Playing," the mastman corrected him. And pointing to a short strip of beach beneath rocky slopes that not even a goat could have climbed, he added, "That's Elephant Seal Beach."

Elephant seals!

Could these bulls, roaring and playfully attacking each other, be the same sea elephants he had seen in the San Diego Zoo? There the bulls, perhaps twenty feet in length, as well as the smaller cows, had lain like long heaps of sacked cement. Only at intervals had they stirred enough to raise clouds of dust when they flapped their flippers to drive away insects.

But when Randy looked at the beach where Lucca was pointing, he saw that the elephant seals of Guadalupe Island were as sluggish on land as those in the zoo. It was past the breeding season and there were few cows or pups here. The bulls lay twitching and quivering as if having troubled dreams, while six others lay in the surf. One would hump forward several feet like a mammoth worm, then fall asleep from the exertion; whereupon another elephant seal would start the same strange humping advance toward dry sand.

Sounds at the stern of the boat now caught Randy's attention. Glancing back, he saw that Riggio and Puccinelli were drawing the smaller skiff closer with the towline. Steve had throttled down the motor of the speedboat and was taking a slow, circling course. Puccinelli passed a line, to which cork floats were attached, to Doc Bernedetto. The chummer slipped it under a thwart, dogged it down securely and then cast off the towrope.

Bernedetto and the plump cook, Terraza, took their places on the thwarts, splashed oars overboard, and began rowing to hold their position. This was difficult, for the small skiff was bobbing like a chip, buffeted by both breakers and ground swells.

Nevertheless, the little boat acted as a drag on the cork line. This line pulled layer after layer of the seine from the stern of the net skiff as the launch towed the boat in a wide circle. The net failed to go overboard rapidly enough, however, so the six men in the boat assisted by tumbling it into the water. So much weight at the stern almost stood the skiff on end, and the awkward angle made it difficult to work. More than once Randy felt a foot crushing his own as he heaved on the heavy net. Frequently he bore down on a fisherman's boot and heard a yell of protest.

Steve had gauged his circle so that the last of the seine splashed overboard just as the net skiff came alongside the smaller one manned by Bernedetto and Terraza.

Doc Bernedetto now untied the cork line, passing it over to Puccinelli. Randy and Louie helped him pull it aboard.

With it came a portion of the net, which they made fast to a thwart. Now the seine net encircled hundreds of beautiful little fish, azure blue in color, all darting and milling in fright. Bernedetto leaned over to grasp a wriggling fish and examine it carefully.

"What are they, Doc?" Steve called from the speedboat.

"Azurinas," said the chummer. "Seldom see them."

"Any good for bait?" inquired Puccinelli.

"If I can keep them alive," said Bernedetto doubtfully.

Someone shouted. Randy turned and saw that the weight of fish in the seine had pulled the cork line at the opposite side under water. Azurinas darted across it to escape.

The speedboat's motor suddenly roared. Steve swung it alongside the small skiff long enough for Terraza to secure a towline. Then the little boat was given a rough, fast passage halfway around the seine. The cook freed the towrope, and then, with the chummer's help, started heaving up the edge of the net until Doc Bernedetto could lash it to a thwart. The drag of the seine nearly pulled the little boat's gunwale under water. But the cork line now formed a perfect circle on the surface, except where it was drawn aboard the two skiffs. No fish could swim over it.

Looking down through the crystal-clear water, Randy saw that the bottom of the net was still open. No azurinas were as yet being lost, however, because the bottom folds rested on big rocks or sand.

Tony Riggio had stripped to his trunks. Now he pulled on rolled-down rubber boots. Puccinelli lifted the copper helmet over the diver's round, bald head. It was a simple rig that extended down over Riggio's shoulders and upper chest, but left his arms free. His other equipment was the lead belt to which his life line was secured, and a knife-sheath.

Riggio eased his short, stocky body over the side but clung to the gunwale until Lucca started to supply air with the tire pump. Releasing his hold then, he grasped his life line so that he might signal while descending, if necessary. When he waved Puccinelli paid out the rope. The helmet slipped under a rolling swell, soon growing indistinct beneath a frothy swirl of rising air bubbles.

Randy knew it was Riggio's job to "purse" the bottom of the net as an inverted hand-bag might be closed by pulling drawstrings. Until that was done, the purse-seine could not be towed out to the *Ripple* without losing its load of sardines. But on rocky bottoms where tuna boats took most of their bait, the net usually snagged at many points; only a diver could free it and draw together and tie the bottom line.

Reaching bottom, Riggio began clambering slowly over big boulders, to free the net where it was caught on projections or in cracks. He was a third of the way around the seine when a fisherman shouted.

Randy's heart faltered as he spied a heavy, grayish form circling the silvery stream of rising air bubbles. Puccinelli jerked the life line attached to Riggio's belt. The stocky little diver ducked under the edge of the net—and not a moment too soon! The elephant seal brushed the webbing a scant two feet from Riggio. Startled by the unfamiliar feel of it, the monster began a rapid ascent.

As it broke water, the animal's humped nose drew back

and it roared. Almost immediately, however, it slipped beneath a surging ground swell to start another dive. Riggio had pulled himself out from under the seine and was grasping it for support as he leaned back, trying to look upward through his oval vision plate. Apparently he failed to see the great beast circling above him. Not until Puccinelli snapped a signal on the line did the diver once more duck under the net for protection.

The elephant seal appeared to be swimming directly toward Riggio where he lay flattened against a slanting rock, but when a flipper touched the cording, the animal swerved away. The diver remained motionless while the seal completed another ascent and again sounded. Three more times it repeated this maneuver of spiraling around the air bubbles, only to be frightened away by the net separating it from Riggio.

When it rose from the last dive, Puccinelli's broad, childlike face was crimson with anger. Dropping the coil of lifeline, he seized an oar and brought it down with a sharp *thwack* on the animal's head. The elephant seal roared with pain and surprise. Then, beating the water into swirls and eddies with its flippers, it vanished in a smother of foam.

Randy saw it making a brief, circling dive. Quickly its head reappeared, rising almost as high as their gunwale. Its short trunk lifted as it gave voice to an indignant roar. Puccinelli had recovered the coil of line, but now he flung it aside to reach for the oar.

Steve Vardon had been sending up a fan of spray as he cut through the big, glassy swells with the speedboat. His efforts to divert the elephant seal's attention were meeting with no success because he could not approach close to the net without entangling the cork line in the boat's propeller.

Now, grasping the giant fisherman's intention, he reduced speed, swerving toward the net skiff. "Don't strike it again, Puccinelli!" he shouted. "It might attack your boat!"

So infuriated that he heard nothing the navigator was saying, the big man brought his wet oar down in a swift, glistening arc. The elephant seal saw the descending wooden blade and started a rolling dive to evade the blow. But not quite in time! The oar struck the animal's shining back and shattered!

Puccinelli stared blankly at his broken weapon. Then with a snort he hurled it overboard.

"Here it comes!" shrieked Louie. "*Hang on!*"

Through the transparent water, Randy saw the long, gray body swiftly rising. The elephant seal was ascending directly toward their boat.

"It—it's going to crash into us!" Randy faltered.

CHAPTER THREE

Elephant Seals Can Be

Too Playful

RANDY COULD not even brace himself well before the elephant seal struck the net skiff. The impact bounced him into the air. When he came down across the gunwale, his midriff took the force of his fall. The breath was knocked from his body, leaving him too stunned to do anything when he felt himself sliding forward into the water.

Most of the fishermen had been hurled from their feet. Only Jack Lucca was in a position to help. He grasped Randy's belt and pulled him back into the skiff.

"Th-thanks," the boy gasped.

"What's it going to do next?" Lucca wondered, leaning over the side.

Though still feeling weak and shaky, Randy also peered down. In a moment the giant seal swam into view. He sensed that it would rise between the ends of the skiff and the speedboat.

The motor of the latter boat was now throttled down. Randy was surprised to see that Ortorio had taken the wheel. Steve Vardon was standing, legs wide braced, an automatic pistol in his hand. It was pointed at an angle that would allow a bullet, should it ricochet, to pass harmlessly by the end of the skiff. Randy had wondered why the navigator had strapped on a holster before stepping into the boat. Now he realized that it was to meet just such an emergency as this one.

But was this man, waiting with leveled gun, the same good-natured navigator who was teaching him to steer the *Ripple?* A change had come over Steve, to make him as unfamiliar as a stranger. His expression was coldly remote, his eyes had a frosty glimmer. In a moment the explanation occurred to Randy. This must be the other side of his friend! This was the Steve Vardon who had fought without quarter in the skies of Germany and the South Pacific, who had flown through Alaskan snowstorms and the blizzards of the high Andes.

The automatic cracked twice as the seal's glossy head broke water. Two bullets whined over the animal to strike a flowing swell with a muffled *pung-pung*. Startled cormorants and pelicans beat the air with strong wings as they left the water, scattering feathers behind.

The elephant seal did not delay to learn the cause of the explosions. It lashed the water into gleaming spray in its sudden dive. Randy watched it sculling away with its powerful flippers as it descended on a curving course to avoid the net. Then it vanished into the depths.

"Why didn't you shoot it?" demanded Puccinelli.

"Because these seals are protected by law," growled Steve. "Besides, it probably meant no harm. By stirring it up, Puccinelli, you might have caused us to lose our net and bait. Or even some men!"

The big fisherman had an injured expression. "It was after Riggio!"

"He was safe," said Steve, snapping the weapon back into its holster. "Tug his line, and see if he wants to come up."

At the signal, Riggio crawled out from between two rocks where he had taken refuge. He answered with a single jerk of his line to say he intended to continue his work.

Within half an hour he had drawn the bottom of the net together on a patch of sand, and "pursed" it by pulling in the line and tying it. Puccinelli then hauled him up with the life line.

Once more Steve took the net skiff in tow. The speed-boat circled slowly, for the larger skiff was partially supporting a net weighed with small fish. The smaller boat, which shared this burden, began swinging around with the movement of the seine; and when it had made a half-circle, Steve began to tow both the loaded net and the skiffs toward the *Ripple*.

As the large skiff was brought alongside the vessel, men scrambled up a Jacob's ladder and began to pull the cork-float line aboard. Randy, toiling with the others, found this heavy work.

"That's enough," declared the skipper, who had been doing his share and more.

Enough webbing was aboard to compress the fish into one side of the seine. This placed great strain on the small skiff, making it tip at a precarious angle. Doc Bernedetto and George Terraza sat on the high gunwale to prevent it from flopping over.

"Hurry up!" Bernedetto urged. "We're about to turn

turtle."

Louie ran for the long-poled scoop, which had a hoop and a small net on one end. After passing it to Riggio, he hurried to the nearest bait tank to remove the planks covering it, and switched on the overhead globe. Unless a light burned over the tank, Randy recalled, the sardines would mill in every direction, lose their scales and soon die.

Riggio dipped the scoop into the seine, bringing it up wriggling with small fish that blazed azure-blue and silver in the dazzling sunlight. He pushed the long handle back to Louie, who was now on the ladder. The captain's son dumped the little fish into the bait tank. This operation continued until Riggio was raising the scoop half-empty. Then it was necessary to shorten the seine by drawing more net aboard in order to take the remaining chums.

"One hundred and eight scoops," Louie reported.

"Not too good," observed Riggio. "Wonder if we'll get any more."

Randy saw that only a few birds were still wheeling under the cliffs. Around the ship, however, and under the steep hang of the northern hook of the cove there were many birds in the air and on the water. Their first set of the net, the boy realized, had scattered the azurinas away from the shallows.

Nevertheless, the net was piled into the larger skiff, and Steve once more towed the boats across the cove to make a second set. It was done as before, but this time fewer fish flopped within the circle of cork floats. Riggio pursed the seine, and it was brought back to the clipper.

The captain looked down to see what it might hold. "Not

more than forty scoops. We might as well pull out of here."
He glanced toward Steve, who had brought the speedboat to
a stop at the *Ripple's* stern. "Like to get us some fresh meat?"

The navigator looked quickly toward the cliffs—straight
walls of bare rock, plunging several thousand feet from the
flanks of the mountains above.

"No goat could scale that cliff," said Castignoni. "Sail to
Northeast Anchorage, and we'll pick you up when we've
taken our bait."

"Joe," said Ortorio with dignity, "I must refuse. My last
climb on this island nearly finished me."

"No, it's too rugged for you." And looking over the men
heaving the net aboard, the captain spied Randy. "You go
along and help pack the meat."

Steve chugged in closer to the low stern so that Ortorio
could climb aboard the *Ripple*. Then Randy dropped into
the speedboat. He was glad enough to go. But he was aware
that he had once more been chosen for a hard job. What had
he done to arouse such antagonism in the skipper?

Castignoni returned with a heavy tarpaulin, a large knife,
a rifle and a box of cartridges, which he handed down. "Don't
go too far, Steve."

The navigator nodded and opened the trottle. The speedboat headed out toward the entrance. There, where she encountered the ocean swells in her northward turn, spray began breaking in iridescent clouds over her bow. The boat
pounded along past talus slopes and black volcanic cliffs,
while the seas shattered along the base of the island in explosions of spindrift.

Uneasily Randy glanced at Steve. "What if our motor stops?"

A faint, ironical smile lighted the navigator's spray-damp face. Jerking a thumb downward, he made a gurgling sound. "What to live forever?" he yelled cheerfully.

"Sure," replied Randy with a pallid grin.

The boy's stomach tightened as the big swells battered the boat, at times almost rolling it onto its beam ends. He knew Steve was right. Nothing could save them if they capsized here.

He was relieved when at length the boat fought through the seas churning around North Point. Once the massive headland lay astern, they were in the lee of the island, speeding along through lazy rollers. For more than a mile they skirted the eastern shoreline. Then there was a break in the high palisades, and Steve turned toward it. The boat clapped and bounded through water boiling and rippling like a mountain torrent. But presently the entrance lay behind. They glided through swells that flashed like mercury in the play of sunlight.

Randy saw that they were in a high-walled cove. Directly ahead a heavy surf crashed in great white breakers against a steep beach. Steve was turning the speedboat toward the southeastern part of the bay. There, beneath the sparsely grassed slope of a towering mountain, was a graveled beach, washed by a light surf. Above the black lava rocks of the beach and sheltered in a small valley, stood several small wooden dwellings and one of larger size, double-storied, of white stucco.

"Did someone have a ranch here?" Randy inquired curiously.

"The Mexicans once established a barracks here," replied Steve. "After it was abandoned, a Mexican outfit brought goats to this cove and canned the meat in the larger building. When the venture lost money the goats were left to shift for themselves. They've multiplied and wandered all over Guadalupe in search of food. Now there's hardly a young tree or a blade of grass on the island. There never was much water here, except for seepage on the higher slopes, so the goats come down to the sea to drink during droughts."

"Wouldn't sea water kill them?"

"Not goats," answered Steve. "Even humans can make out with forty per cent brine mixed with fresh water, if they have to."

Skillfully Steve wove between the rocks, now protruding from the shoaling water, and shut off the motor. Randy jumped forward to pick up the mooring line. He sprang ashore as the boat grated on the beach.

Steve loaded the rifle, dropped some shells into his shirt pocket and stepped out.

More than a dozen goats were grazing on tufts of short brown grass growing between the outcrops of lava on the slopes above them. They raised their heads to stare down at the strangers.

Steve raised his rifle, then lowered it. "Like shooting your own cow!" he said disgustedly. "Let's at least give them a chance."

Picking up a rock, he hurled it far up the mountain side.

It fell yards short of the nearest animal. The goat bounded away as if on springs. Instantly the others imitated its example.

Steve threw the rifle to his shoulder, took quick aim and squeezed the trigger. A young goat was springing from an outcrop when the shot rang out; it crumpled as it landed on another spur of rock. Even before it struck the ground, the rifle cracked a second time. Another goat, climbing a shale slope, suddenly dropped and began to slide in a small cascade of rubble. Steve snapped out three more fast shots, and two goats tumbled and rolled from the side of a small pinnacle. Every other animal had vanished.

"Blamed if I don't hate to kill anything!" Steve muttered as he reloaded.

Randy glanced in surprise at this man who had more than once downed enemy planes in combat. Steve saw the unspoken question in the boy's eyes. "When it's an enemy's life or yours, Randy, it's different."

"Won't the goats starve if they're not thinned out?"

"That's a fact," said Steve, starting on.

They passed the barracks and several shacks with missing doors and broken windows, to enter a narrow gulley. Steve climbed at a steady, tireless pace that did not appear fast but covered ground quickly. When they left the depression and came out upon a sloping face of the mountain, Randy was breathing hard. Steve pointed out two crumpled forms half-covered with shale.

"There are the last two. With high meat prices this helps keep our expenses low, Randy. And since we fish on shares, it means a more profitable cruise. You take one; I'll pack the other."

Hoisting the young goats to their shoulders, they trudged to the beach with them. A return trip had to be made for the other two. Steve butchered the four animals, and Randy stowed the meat in the speedboat, covering it with the tarp. Then the navigator glanced at his wristwatch. "Still time to do a little more hunting."

They climbed high up the shoulder of the mountain, to a gap in a ridge. Behind them the abandoned buildings of the old Mexican barracks had dwindled to the size of postage stamps. To the eastward, the mountain dipped into a short valley before rising once more in a steep pitch.

"Good observation point," said Steve. "Let's sit down and wait."

Randy was almost gasping for breath. But he managed to point out five goats watching them from the valley below. All were gaunt animals.

"T-too old?" he asked.

Steve nodded. "They'd be tough and stringy. Not worth packing back."

Randy dropped flat on the ground. In a few minutes he was breathing normally and sat up. "Won't you tell me something about Frank's Uncle Vittorio?"

Steve's eyes crinkled humorously. "You must know him as well as I do. I made only one cruise on the *Westwind*, remember."

"But I met him only at family parties," Randy explained. "He was pleasant and had a sort of old-fashioned courtesy.

· 55 ·

He struck you as foreign, while Frank's dad, our skipper, might have been born here."

"Vittorio Castignoni was twenty years older than his brother Joe when they came to America together," Steve commented. "They tried different types of fishing, then got into the tuna game when it was in its infancy, back in the early thirties. Joe was more venturesome, and it was he who first bought a tuna boat. A pretty poor little craft, from what I've heard, but she made money. Then he helped Vittorio buy one. They assisted one another in buying better and better boats, until Joe owned the *Ripple* and Vittorio, the *Westwind*."

Steve paused, raising his rifle as a young goat, scarcely more than a kid, appeared from a small valley to seaward. His weapon made a sharp *crack*. The goat fell, rolling over to drop from sight into an *arroyo*.

"We'll pick it up later," Steve said. He turned searching eyes on the boy. "Why are you questioning me about Vittorio Castignoni?"

"It might give me a clue to how the *Westwind* disappeared."

Steve shook his head. "I don't know him well enough to help you much that way, Randy."

After scanning the valleys and mountains for several minutes, the navigator chuckled. "Vittorio clung to Old World customs, way of thinking and habits of thrift," he recalled. "Without the flick of an eyelash he'd spend twenty or thirty thousand dollars overhauling his boat, yet he'd raise an awful ruckus if one of us cast overboard an old piece of rope that might still be used. He'd been so poor as a boy in Italy that he couldn't bear waste, and as a result he became a regular marine junkman."

"How do you mean, Steve?"

"Well, he was always picking up anything afloat or from beaches that he might use himself or sell at salvage yards. Oil drums he could turn in for a $3.50 refund. Old lengths of hawser. Worn-out brushes. Rusting pieces of machinery he'd find left on some lonely strand and could dispose of as scrap metal. All storage space on the *Westwind* was cluttered up with such stuff."

"It must have cost more to transport than it was worth!"

"Probably did," Steve agreed. "But I'll never forget the big, broken spar he fished from the sea and stowed beside the bait tanks. We stumbled over it every time we went aft. Or, if we didn't, we'd pretend we had, just so we could beef about it.

"Then one day when we were in a squall, the chummer had the bad judgment to go and see how his bait was taking the heavy seas. We were riding heavy, with over a hundred tons of tuna in the wells and the after-deck all awash from midships to the taffrail. A roaring wash crashed over the well deck, sweeping the chummer overboard.

"Luckily, he was missed within a few minutes. Castignoni hauled the clipper around and we sailed back and found the man. By rising on the crests and diving when the seas were breaking over him, he'd stayed afloat, but he looked sort of water-logged. Five of us were lowered in the speedboat and we picked up the chummer without much trouble. But the clipper was rolling so much that our boat would have been smashed if we'd run alongside to be taken up on the falls.

"Vittorio Castignoni saw he might lose all six of us. So he put the *Westwind* on the 'Iron Mike'—on automatic control—and ran aft to direct the fishermen in preparing some kind of rescue gear. With the seas smashing over the well deck, we couldn't see what they were doing, but we expected the men to be washed over at any minute. Then the stern lifted a little, and we saw the skipper signaling us to come closer. Risky as it was, we crept in near enough to grab a line he cast to us. We didn't know what to do with it until the men on board tumbled over a whole mess of stuff. From that broken spar, bamboo poles and a big piece of salvaged canvas and ropes, Castignoni had rigged up a triangular raft. When we took this sea-anchor in tow it acted as a drag to hold our stern in the water, and we were able to head into the seas. Castignoni maneuvered the clipper to shelter us from the wind and give us a lee, too, so that we rode out the squall. After conditions had moderated, we were taken aboard.

"Every man of us wanted to salvage the spar. But remembering how much grumbling it had caused, Vittorio said, 'No, it has done its work.' After we were under way again, however, he walked out onto the bridge wing to look back with regret at the drifting spar and poles and canvas. Waste always distressed him. For the remainder of the cruise, he could have stopped for a strawberry crate and not a man would have let out a murmur." There was a warm note of admiration in Steve's voice as he added, "That Old Man was sea-wise, and plenty salty!"

As he concluded, he peered at an outcrop of rock to the eastward, then slowly raised the rifle. Two goats had ventured from hiding. When both were in view Steve fired. A split-second later he snapped out a second shot. The nearer goat staggered and dropped, but the other one bounded for cover and escaped. The second bullet ricocheted from a rock with a high-pitched wailing sound.

"Old age has overtaken me!" lamented Steve. He reloaded and handed the weapon to Randy. "See what you can do."

Randy had often practised target shooting on his desert camping trips with Frank Castignoni, but he wasn't sure he could hit a live object. All the animals had vanished, even the old billy goats in the valley. A minute later the one that had escaped Steve's last shot climbed onto a rocky knoll, apparently curious about the sounds that had caused its fright.

Randy pressed steadily on the trigger. His ears rang from the explosion, and his right shoulder was wrenched by the swift recoil of the rifle. The goat plunged from the rock and landed at its base, still kicking. Feeling suddenly ill, Randy thrust the gun at Steve. "Oh, Steve—kill it! It's only wounded!"

Steve shook his head and laid the rifle across his knees. The animal's jerking had ceased and it now lay motionless.

"Reflex movements, Randy. It was dead when it hit the ground." Rising, he said, "We'd better get the carcasses dressed so we won't delay the boat."

They recovered the last two animals shot and plodded back to the beach. While Steve was butchering them, Randy set out to bring in the third goat.

As he returned with it he thought of what Steve had told him of Vittorio Castignoni. Though he better understood Frank's uncle now, nothing he had learned seemed useful. Randy didn't realize then that Steve had given him a clue which, in the weeks to come, would help to part the veil of mystery surrounding the clipper *Westwind*. . . .

The meat from their seven goats was in the speedboat by the time the *Ripple* sailed into the bay. Steve set out immediately to meet her, and a few minutes later the boat was taken aboard.

"Terraza will finish butchering and stow our 'mutton' in the freeze room, Randy," Steve declared as he stepped out on deck. "Let's get cleaned up."

Randy had taken a shower and had changed into clean clothes when Louie appeared to inform him that the skipper wanted him on the bridge.

Climbing the mountainous slopes of the island, packing meat and hauling on the seine had left Randy sore and tired. The captain must realize that he had asked more of the boy than of any man aboard.

For a moment resentment flared in him. Then he remembered that Castignoni had given him a chance to find Frank. The captain had kept his part of their bargain. Now Randy intended to keep his, no matter how unreasonable the skipper might be.

The *Ripple* was well to the eastward of Guadalupe Island and sailing southward, when Randy reached the wheelhouse.

Captain Castignoni was on his high stool beside the window, staring out at the cliffs slipping by to starboard. The wheel clicked under the control of the gyro-steering device and it was clear that no helmsman was needed.

Nevertheless, Castignoni said gruffly, "Relieve the Iron Mike."

Randy released the controls and took the wheel. He managed to steer a straighter course than on previous occasions, though he still found it hard to keep the gyro-compass needle where it belonged. Every deviation from their course brought a sharp rebuke from the skipper.

The boat sailed southward along mountains of diminishing stature for nearly two hours. And then, when she was only a little over a mile from the southern tip of the island, the captain left his stool. He pointed to a cloud of pelicans and cormorants appearing and vanishing into a recess in the bluffs.

"Looks like we might take more sardines. Get something to eat."

In the galley Randy found George Terraza making preparations for dinner. "We're going to start seining in a few minutes," the boy announced. "I haven't eaten since breakfast. Can I get a bite?"

The plump cook pointed to a plate of meat and cheese and a platter of bread on the table. "Eat hearty, kid. Wouldn't surprise me if we're still scooping bait at four tomorrow morning."

The cook's prediction proved right!

Randy and the other men made their initial set of the seine

net as the shadows were spilling down the low bluffs surrounding the southeast anchorage. It was dark when the first azurinas were transferred to the bait tank. The boats nevertheless toiled on through the night. To avoid frightening the fish, the men worked in a darkness relieved only by the phosphorescent flashing of sardines in the net, the faint illumination from the anchorage light and the small globe burning over the bait boxes. Three sets were made before the scattering of azurinas made further seining unprofitable.

The *Ripple* carried nearly five hundred scoops of chums in her tanks when she sailed from the cove. Randy leaned wearily on the rail as she turned southward. Off to port he made out the pale outline of mountains against the lightening sky, but the moon was still high enough to turn the sea to quicksilver. Numb with exhaustion, he turned into his room, climbed onto his bunk without bothering to remove his clothing, and promptly fell into a dreamless sleep.

He was still so sleepy when he joined the men in the galley the next morning that he failed to notice the cook heaping his plate twice after he had eaten his original helping. He wondered why it took so long to finish.

More drowsy than before, he stumbled out to where the fishermen were working on their gear under the main-deck overhang. Guadalupe Island had vanished to the north, and the clipper was so far out to sea that the mountains of Lower California looked as soft as brown velvet. The light breeze scarcely riffled the mirrored water. The purr of the Diesels, the faint musical hissing of water along the hull and the balmy air had a lulling effect. Randy lay down on a hatch and was soon fast asleep.

A hot sun blazed overhead when he awakened. Most of the men, he saw, had left to wash up for lunch. When he walked aft along the well deck, however, he spied Jack Lucca high in the crow's nest, scanning the horizon, and Steve Vardon was removing the tarp from the scouting plane on the bait-tank canopy.

Randy went to help stow away the tarpaulin, and then he watched Steve checking the plane for signs of salt-water corrosion. "Going to look for tuna, Steve?"

"After lunch, I will."

It suddenly occurred to Randy that a fellow flying several thousand feet in altitude could scan the sea for a vast distance in every direction. He'd have a chance to spot any wreckage afloat. And he might see a smoke signal, if any were being sent up by survivors of the *Westwind* from this barren stretch of coast.

"Could I go with you, Steve?" Randy asked eagerly.

Steve's eyes crinkled as he looked at the tall and solidly built boy peering so anxiously at him. "Ask the Old Man."

Randy dashed up to the bridge. Captain Castignoni stared moodily across the sea while the automatic pilot guided the boat. The boy made his request in a voice that shook with excitement. His heart thumped with heavy beats as he awaited the captain's reply.

"Two pairs of eyes might be better than one," the skipper at length conceded. "Take those binoculars up there."

"Thank you, Captain!" Randy cried in relief. He started toward the door, then turned, a delighted smile lighting his face. "I've never been up in a plane before."

He was too keyed up to eat much lunch. Passing up dessert, he hurried aft to the bait tank, where Steve still worked on the engine.

"Get your wool cap and pea-jacket," Steve advised. "You'll find it cooler aloft than you think."

The navigator had completed his check-up when Randy returned. "Hop in," he said. "We're all set."

The throb of the *Ripple's* engines had faded to a low humming and she was drifting to a stop, when Randy clambered into the tiny cabin. He settled himself into the soft, foam-rubber seat and buckled on his safety belt. William McDowd appeared to start the winch. He dropped the boom so that Steve could secure a pair of cables and slip hooks through lifting-rings on the plane's wings.

Then Steve stepped inside, slammed the door, took his place at the controls and strapped on his helmet. Sliding back a window, he yelled, "Hoist away, Chief."

Randy felt a quiver of excitement when the boom began to creak and the cables rasped. Slowly the plane was raised from the chocks and swung around, until the boy could look down from a window upon the light swells slapping the boat's side. Down they dropped then, striking the water with a splash. Steve climbed out on one wing, then the other, to free the hooks, and then squeezed through the window to slide into his seat once more. At a shout from a fisherman, McDowd lifted the boom.

Steve waited for the clipper to churn water and get under way before he started the plane's motor. It coughed, sputtered and popped, then broke into a roar. He studied his panel gauges as he revved up the engine in snarling spasms. Shrill as a cyclone the wind whistled in through the open window.

Minutes later the motor raised its voice in a loud, defiant roar and the plane began to move. Slowly the pontoons overcame water suction. Harshly they clapped, making the plane tremble as it picked up speed. Spray hailed against the fuselage and flew past the windows in driving showers.

Abruptly the noise ceased. The plane wobbled free, its roar changing to a high-pitched drone. Randy's throat was choked up with excitement. For a moment he pressed his face to the window to look down upon the bright water flowing under their wings. The intensified drone of the motor told him the plane was fighting for altitude. Yet it seemed a long time to the boy before he felt sure they were climbing safely toward the shining blue vault of the sky.

When he looked down again the sea had flattened out like a sheet of hammered silver, thousands of feet below. Randy remembered the binoculars then, and removed them from the case. He scanned the Mexican coast, with its long white beach below high, rocky bluffs. Far beyond the coast the craggy chain of mountains were shimmering in the heat waves. Randy turned his glass back to the beach, sweeping it to north and south, but without finding any sign of wreckage or a camp along the desolate shore.

As the plane began banking he brought the glass to bear on the *Ripple*. She had a bone in her teeth where her cutwater cleaved the glassy sea. Astern of her lay the white ribbon of her wake.

Presently Randy realized that Steve had begun to circle the boat. In a wide sweep they buzzed near the Mexican shoreline, swung on a curving course to the south and then the west, with the mother vessel never more than ten miles distant. But when they had completed the first circle Steve flew farther southward to increase their visual range by a larger spiraling flight.

They were making their fourth cycle, perhaps twenty miles to the south of the *Ripple,* when Randy made out a lacy-white line with his glass. As the plane drew nearer the roiled water, he could distinguish an advancing column of what at first appeared to be small fish, their bodies glistening black against the sparkling water. "Look, Steve," he shouted, putting a hand on the pilot's shoulder. "A school of porpoises!"

Steve looked back with a startled glance. "Are they carrying tuna?"

Randy flushed at the question and raised his glass again. What a dumbbell he was! Any tuna fisherman's son should remember that porpoises fed on the same small fish as yellowfins and skipjacks! When they were together, porpoises were said to be "carrying a school of tuna."

Now, feeling slightly foolish, Randy studied the leaping porpoises more carefully. Sure enough! Behind the small animals lay ruffled water. And now he observed small, whirling dots above the sea, that must be birds.

He reported his discovery. Steve nodded and switched on the short-wave radio. There was a squawk, a crackle of static. Then a voice filtered through the bellow of the engine.

"Hear me, Joe?" Steve yelled into the speaker. "Randy spotted porpoises carrying you know what. Over." Again Randy made out a voice, though he couldn't catch the words. "Okay," Steve answered. "Bear south by southwest, Joe. We're coming in."

Randy's heart-beat quickened as the plane banked. For the first time in his life he might soon be fishing for tuna!

CHAPTER FOUR

The Fighting Fury of

Four-Pole Tuna

THE PLANE'S nose dipped, making earth and sky and water tilt sharply. Then they were diving at a speed that caused Randy's muscles to tighten in alarm. The slip-stream blew a gale through the open window. He felt the trembling of the little hydroplane each time Steve gunned the popping motor to prevent it from flooding.

Towing a pale-green patch of boiling water astern, the *Ripple* grew rapidly larger to the northwest. While still several miles from her, however, Steve leveled out, and the flashing swells streamed under their wings. Momentary panic stirred in the boy when the plane struck and bounded into the air. Twice more it smacked the surface and bounced. Then the pontoons were clapping, while to right and left appeared rainbow veils of spray. Water beat with a loud patter on the plane's underside as it taxied toward the approaching tuna clipper. Steve shut off the motor, and the hydroplane drifted to a stop in the lazy rollers.

When he glanced back Randy grinned. "You sure know your job!"

Steve laughed. "This is tame compared with flying

through rain, snow and sleet in Alaska. The fogs up there were full of mountains, and you had few lights to guide you. Mostly you followed rivers or ranges, and hoped they were the right ones. I certainly earned the two thousand dollars a month they paid me!"

"Two thousand!" Randy exclaimed "The weather must have been rugged to give up that job!"

"It wasn't the weather. I was becoming too fond of a swell kid in the airport office at Anchorage. I decided to move on before we got married."

"What's wrong with that?" Randy asked in astonishment.

"Unfair to the girl," Steve said shortly. "Wandering feet like mine don't go with marriage."

Randy was puzzled. He knew Steve had unusual ability and could turn his hand to almost anything. But he had also discovered in their talks together that Steve had held eight jobs since leaving the service. How could he ever put down permanent roots if he never stuck at anything long enough to make a success of it?

"Time to secure," observed Steve. And the plane rocked as he wriggled through the window onto the right wing.

The *Ripple* slowly bore down to windward, her boom once more swung over the side. Steve grasped the dangling hooks, slipping one through each lifting-ring. Then he climbed back into his seat. "Heave away!" he shouted.

With a noisy grating the cable drew the little hydroplane upward and then swung it around jerkily, until it hovered over the bait tank canopy. Four fishermen were there to guide it into the big V-shaped chocks as it was lowered. Once the plane was securely lashed in place, the vessel got under way and the men left Randy and Steve to pull on the tarps.

When this was done, they slid down from the canopy to the edge of the tank. Doc Bernedetto and Freshwater stood on the ladders at opposite sides of the box. They were forcing azurinas over to the port side with a "crowder"—a net stretched between two bamboo poles which reached from top to bottom of the tank. Randy had heard that a crowder was a useful means of confining sardines within a smaller space so they could be scooped out more easily by a chummer.

Steve peered down into the tank. "You've got a lot of dead ones down there, Doc."

Bernedetto nodded. "I'll siphon them out later. This is weak bait and won't last long."

Randy heard a commotion on deck and turned to see Nicco Puccinelli lifting Julio Ortorio by his armpits. The little man's white mustache twitched with indignation; his black eyes were snapping.

"Here's some good bait, Doc," yelled Puccinelli.

"Let me down!" sputtered Ortorio.

Puccinelli grinned broadly as he set Ortorio down carefully. The little man shook his fist at his friend. "Beware!" he piped shrilly. "My patience is near an end. Some day I will take stern measures!"

His threat brought a roar of laughter from the fishermen on deck. Outraged by this fresh affront of his dignity, Ortorio stalked away.

Randy realized the men intended no offense; they were in unusually high spirits because of the possibility of taking tuna early in the cruise. George Terraza left the galley and began slapping the rail with his plump palms while he chanted a Mexican song, sadly off key. Louie was playing idly with his silver bracelet and smiling to himself. Tony Riggio began to dance a rumba with an imaginary partner. The others clapped and stomped.

Soon tiring of his dance, Riggio shouted at the mastman to tell more about the school of tuna. Jack Lucca continued to peer southward through his glass without answering. Puccinelli strode over to grasp the rope ladder, and drew his legs up quickly so that his descending weight made the mast tremble.

Lucca looked down in alarm. "Stop it, Nicco! You're shaking my glass!"

"That woke him up," exulted Puccinelli happily.

"What do you see?" demanded Riggio.

"A porpoise school about a mile long."

"Can you tell how big the fish are yet?"

A shy smile flitted across the mastman's face and he asked innocently, "How will we take fourteen-pole tuna with a twelve-man crew?"

"*Bah!*" snorted Riggio. "Who ever heard of fourteen-pole tuna! We'll see for ourselves!"

The men dashed forward, up the ladder and around the deck outside of the wheelhouse. Randy lowered himself down a drain pipe, and when he reached the bridge the fishermen were staring intently across the silvered sheet of water. Below a cloud of wheeling birds lay a patch of ruffled sea, briefly lighted here and there where fish broke the surface.

Beyond the disturbed area porpoises leaped and splashed in pursuit of small fish that at times left the water in their effort to escape.

"We might take fifty tons from this school," declared Freshwater.

"Speak not of good luck so early," reproved Ortorio, who had come to join them.

"That is true," agreed Puccinelli. "These fish may not bite."

"Or if they do," added Ortorio, "they will be too small to keep."

Randy glanced around in surprise. Puccinelli and Ortorio did not look gloomy; their faces glowed with excitement. He decided they were following an Old World ritual for insuring good luck by speaking of bad.

The fishermen watched the roughened water ahead with poor patience. But they could do nothing until the mastman saw the first fish and announced its size. Then the men would know what poles were needed, for the tuna in a school usually varied little in either weight or length.

Suddenly Lucca's voice rang out. "Four-polers, boys!"

Men jostled each other as they crowded toward the ladder, then pounded across the main deck to drop down another. Some broke out poles stored on brackets under the bait-tank canopy. Others raised the three iron fishing racks turned in against the portside of the tanks, swinging them overboard, so that the sea rippled across the grilled bottoms. Each rack had a low rail on the seaward side, providing support for a fisherman's knee when he was landing fish.

There was little confusion. Each man knew in advance who his teammates would be in taking the larger two-, three-, and four-pole fish. Freshwater appeared with the four-pole rig Randy's team would use. Louie sharply ordered Randy to return to their room for the red plastic crash helmet he had forgotten. And when the boy was back, he saw that Louie had collected four knee pads and four heavy leather belts. Men were strapping the padded protectors to their left knees, the knee that would rest against the iron rail of the fishing rack, so Randy followed their example. The leather belt which he next buckled on had a deep socket in front where the end of the pole would fit.

"Now let's go over this again," Louie said, twisting the Navajo bracelet on his brown wrist as he spoke. "Freshwater is number one man, on the left. Steve's two. I'm three. And, Randy, you're the anchor man, on the extreme right. That's where the smaller, weaker or newer man stands."

"Why?" asked Randy.

"Because, stupid," Louie snapped ungraciously, "we all swing right in boating tuna, and the man on that end doesn't exert himself quite as much."

Steve Vardon hurried up and quickly strapped on his knee pad and belt. Then Randy and his three teammates scrambled over the rail and dropped onto the rack nearest the stern. Ortorio, for once separated from his big friend, was the anchor man on the second rack; he was fishing with McDowd, Terraza and Riggio. Since Doc Bernedetto must remain on the bait-tank ladder, to scoop up chums and cast them overboard, and there were only three other men, Randy decided that only two teams would be at work. To his surprise, however, Puccinelli and Lucca took their places on the first rack. The skipper, leaving the boat on automatic pilot, slid over the rail between them. They had only a three-pole rig.

"Can three men take four-pole tuna?" Randy demanded.

"When one of them is Puccinelli," Louie replied tartly. "He's as strong as a plow horse."

The clipper glided slowly now, perhaps no more than a knot and a half, the water rippling lightly over the bottom grill on which the men stood. Ahead of the vessel the sea's surface was patterned as if by a heavy rainfall.

Doc Bernedetto dipped his hand net into the tank, bringing forth a scoop of wriggling sardines. These chums he began strewing off to port in a steady stream. The small fish darted under the racks since the bottom of the boat afforded them the only possible shelter. Their swift flight would draw tuna toward the racks—if they were biting.

Watching the small fish streaking for cover, Randy forgot his own part in the affair until Louie snapped, "Wake up, dopey!"

With a start he lowered his pole with the others. Their small feathered jig trailed through the water like a live squid as they moved it first forward, then back.

For seconds the steady rain of chums brought no response. Then, as if from a submarine disturbance, the sea began to simmer. For a hundred, two hundred yards and farther, a seething turmoil was shattering the ocean. Diamond showers of spray glinted blindingly where fish broke the surface, blazing purple and silver in the sunlight. Overhead there was an excited clamor from circling cormorants and pelicans. And through the cloud of feathered fishermen plummeted an alien, a man-of-war bird. Its swift descent so took Randy by surprise that he almost dropped his pole. He watched it pluck an azurina from the sea without alighting, then beat the air with powerful wings to regain altitude.

Suddenly a big yellowfin tuna appeared beyond the rack, followed seconds later by dozens of others. Presently they were swarming in great numbers—milling, darting, crowding one another for space, until some were forced half out of the sea in the press of bodies as they fought for chums. They ignored the artificial squids, on their piano-wire leaders, brushing them aside in their frenzied pursuit of azurinas. The rack, dipping with the gentle rolling of the vessel, was jarred again and again by charging fish. Yet none would touch the lures.

Randy knew this all too often happened. His father had told him that on certain days tuna would take squids; on others, sardines. But there were times when nothing would tempt them. Minutes passed without a strike.

"Let's try live bait," shouted the captain.

"That's the hard way," sighed Louie.

One man from each team climbed over the rail with a set of poles, hurrying up to the stowage bracket for others. Louie returned at a run and vaulted over the rail, shaking the rack with his weight. He examined their poles and passed each man his own. And now, dangling from their leader, was a bare, barbless hook. Louie leaned over to collect some water in his cupped hands, and turned to spill it into a small, specially designed pocket in the side of the vessel. He did this several times until the little metal depression was half-full.

"Let's have them, Doc," he shouted at Bernedetto.

The chummer dipped the long-handled scoop into the tank, and pushed the pole along until Louie could grasp two handfuls of small, flopping fish and drop them into the bait pocket. Louie quickly transferred all but one chum in this way, and the last azurina he slipped onto their hook.

The four fishermen swung their poles together, dropping the chum into the churning school of fish. Almost instantly Randy saw a yellowfin darting toward it. Their poles dipped under a staggering impact. Responding like a single man, they heaved on their bent and creaking poles, using part of the drive of the tuna's strike to swing it upward and to the right in a swift arc. Randy was uncomfortably aware that the fish was almost as heavy as himself. It flashed with purplish and silver lights, tail and body whipping as it streaked by less than a yard from his face. The strain of supporting part of the weight of that struggling fish was so great that he let out a gasp of relief when it cleared the rail. Thumping the side of the bait tank, it dropped free of their hook and began flopping on deck, its tail drumming a sharp rataplan.

"Swing wider, greenhorn!" Louie shouted angrily. "The tail of one of these big fellows could crush in your chest!"

While Louie baited their hook, Randy glanced right. The four fishermen on the next rack were grunting as they sent a flashing, fighting tuna around past Julio Ortorio and over the rail. On the third rack Puccinelli was doing his best to replace two men. The muscles in his enormous brown arms bulged as he and Lucca and the captain pitted their combined strength against a 150-pound fish that was battling with savage fury to escape. When the yellowfin cleared the rail and fell to the deck, Puccinelli pushed out his lips, expelling his breath with a whistling sound.

But now Randy saw a small fish was on their hook. With his teammates, he lashed the chum into the milling school. It had scarcely touched the water before there was a silvery streak near their leader. Their poles arched as the team met the strike. There was a terrible tension in Randy's hands, wrists, arms and back. But this time he swung outward and upward in a rotating motion, keeping the jerking tuna well clear of his body when it traced a glittering trajectory past him to skim over the rail.

All four jerked their poles to free the hook, but the yellowfin had swallowed the chum and they couldn't disengage it. Louie pulled himself over the rail and drew his knife. He dared not approach the fish, however, until it had stopped flopping. And while waiting for this to happen the next team boated a fish, forcing Louie to leap aside to avoid being struck by it. Seconds later he ducked to escape a second mishap when the third team lost a fish and the big hook whizzed back with a *thwack* against the bait tank. Darting in quickly then, Louie killed their yellowfin and recovered the hook.

"Bait fishing!" he growled, returning to the rack. "Keep an eye on me, Randy, and don't grow impatient. After I've removed several hooks, you'll have your chance to try it."

Randy shivered, for it seemed to him that anyone stepping

behind the racks risked serious injury.

At first there were excited cries when fish were brought aboard. Before long no one could spare breath for useless talk. The men settled down to the grim contest between human endurance and the great strength of the fish they were landing.

The test was unusually severe for Randy. With better luck he might have become hardened to the ordeal by fishing for one- or even two-pole tuna his first few times on the rack. Such fish required less strength and co-ordination. But when four men united their efforts, timing must be as accurate as for a team of tumblers. If Randy, now fast tiring from the heavy and unfamiliar work, were slow in meeting a strike, undue strain would be placed on the other three poles. And if they should crack, the entire weight of the fish would then fall upon his pole. He'd be catapulted overboard before he realized what had happened!

That was something he dreaded more with every passing minute. Fish blood and slime flowing from the stern of the boat had attracted sharks. And now he saw their gray fins slicing through the water between the close-packed bodies of yellowfin. Sometimes when one of these monsters turned to take bait the chummer had strewn on the ocean, Randy had an appalling glimpse of its traverse mouth, armed with vicious teeth. More than once he saw sharks beating the water to foam with their powerful tails as they dashed in to attack hooked tuna. Later his team was raising a yellowfin when a shark appeared and snatched half of the fish.

"They're getting too bold," Steve growled.

With a shout at the others to stop fishing, he went aft, and returned presently with a shotgun. Louie cut off a chunk of their ruined fish and swung it out temptingly over the water. Steve dropped to the rack beside him, ramming the butt of the gun hard against his shoulder. In a few moments a white-tipped shark thrust up its ugly head to seize the bait. Steve's gun roared twice. Riddled by shot, the monster sank. The water churned and rippled as other sharks attacked their dead companion. Slowly the clipper left them astern.

Before Steve could return the shotgun to the captain's cabin and resume fishing again, however, gray fins once more cleaved the surface.

"It's no use, Steve," Freshwater observed a little later, as another monster almost captured a fish they were swinging aboard. "Sharks go with tuna fishing as corned beef goes with cabbage."

Randy failed to appreciate the humor, for the blood of the shark Steve had killed had attracted others. He knew he must unfailingly time his efforts with those of Steve, Freshwater and Louie to avoid being pulled down among the terrible creatures.

This became increasingly difficult. Staring at the flashing, seething water had a hypnotic effect, so that at times he toiled for minutes without being fully conscious of what he was doing. Muscles never before tried by labor such as this began to ache. His back, his arms at first hurt as from a fresh injury, then finally grew numb. He worked in a daze of fatigue, mechanically lifting and swinging with the others, driving himself to match their movements during moments of mental clarity. It was not in Randy's nature, however, to ask for special consideration, even though this new type of exertion was particularly hard for him.

When it seemed as if he couldn't raise his arms again, the captain shouted, "Wait, boys. We're losing the school."

Randy sagged heavily against the hull. Only a few fish were taking the chums Bernedetto cast overboard, and to his light-shot eyes these yellowfins were nothing more than flashing streaks. The men stopped fishing. The drag of a large tuna while the clipper was making any speed would prove too great a strain for their poles or strength.

Presently the Diesel engines rumbled. Water swished over the racks, streaming by in a silvery current.

"I'd like a rest," Steve admitted, his voice sounding tired. "But fish are piled to the rail. We'd better stach them away before we take more."

With a chorus of groans the men turned and climbed wearily back on deck. Freshwater and Riggio removed the cover from a hatch. For many hours an auxiliary pump had been circulating brine and ammonia through the coiled pipes lining the fish well, and now the hold was chilled below freezing temperature. The men began to slide the tuna along deck and drop them into the well. As the last one was disposed of, the clipper started to lose momentum. Freshwater and Riggio replaced the hatch cover.

Once more there were blinding flashes as yellowfins darted in pursuit of chums. Captain Castignoni had found the school. Fishermen slid over the rail. Racks clattered. Poles were raised; and everyone resumed fishing.

The brief interruption had done Randy little good. As sore muscles were wrenched by sudden impacts on his pole and the frantic jerking of fish, he had to goad himself to take the punishment. Once, when Louie was baiting the hook, Steve noticed the boy's drawn expression and asked whether he'd like to rest. Randy's jaw stiffened and he shook his head.

Half an hour after that he was lifting a fish, when his arms suddenly went lifeless. The fish flopped wildly as it swung toward him, but he was helpless to exert any force on his pole. Though the yellowfin nearly grazed his side, its lashing tail somehow missed him. And instead of the blow Randy expected, there was a searing streak of pain as though a burning iron were passing across his cheek. Ignoring the smarting sensation, he jerked his pole with the others to free the hook, for a little of his strength had returned.

Louie started boosting himself to the rail, then stopped midway, one toe on the bait-pocket. "Well, what do you know!" he exclaimed. "The hook went right through its jaw." Dropping to the rack, he withdrew his knife, handing it to Randy. "Here's an easy one. Watch it, though."

Randy was reaching for the knife when Louie's dark eyes abruptly widened. "What did you do to your face?"

"The fin of that last tuna scratched me," Randy admitted.

"*Fin!*" shouted Louie. "More likely it was the hook! Didn't I tell you to put more oomph into your swing!"

His angry voice attracted men on the other racks. They stopped fishing to stare at Randy. The boy flushed and rubbed his cheek. Withdrawing his hand, he was surprised to see blood on his fingers.

· 81 ·

Captain Castignoni handed his pole to Lucca, and, his face set in stern lines, pushed past the fishermen on the second rack. "How'd that happen?" he asked brusquely.

Randy murmured, "I didn't hold the fish far enough away."

"Why?" demanded Castignoni gruffly. "Getting tired?"

"A—a little, sir."

"Then say so! Ask for a rest when you need it; under-stand?" The skipper wheeled. "Puccinelli, take Randy's place here." He reached for the rail, saying to the boy, "Now come with me."

Clearly the skipper was displeased! But why was he making so much fuss about a mere scratch, Randy wondered, as he followed the captain to his room.

"Scrub that face hard," Castignoni ordered, pointing to the wash basin. "Fish slime can cause a bad infection."

While Randy washed the captain opened a metal first-aid box. From it he removed a bottle of iodine, rolls of sterile gauze and adhesive tape and a small pair of scissors. Then he scrubbed his hands vigorously before cutting off several strips of gauze and tape. It seemed to the boy that the skipper was unnecessarily severe. The mirror had shown only a shallow gash.

"Stand here where the light's good," the captain said gruffly.

Randy flinched at the antiseptic. After applying a generous amount, Castignoni taped gauze over the wound. "Ever notice that white scar on Ortorio's right cheek?" he asked.

"Yes, sir."

"He got it live-bait fishing for four-polers the way we're doing today," explained the captain. "His team caught a big yellowfin through the jaw, and when the men were struggling to boat the fish Ortorio was too exhausted to hold the tuna away. His three big partners didn't see the hook slip between Ortorio's parted lips, and their final heave flung both their anchor man and the fish over the rail. Removing the hook from our mate's cheek was one tough job!"

Randy swallowed when he realized how close he had come to a similar mishap. Small wonder the captain was annoyed with him!

"I don't want to treat another injury like that," the captain went on. "So be more careful."

Footsteps sounded in the wheelhouse and Steve appeared. "We've drifted out of the school again, Joe."

When the two men strode out to the bridge wing, Randy trailed behind. Nowhere was the surface disturbed, except to the south, where porpoises were frolicking.

"It's my hunch the school has sounded, Steve. I wish someone could figure out why tuna will suddenly stop feeding." The captain raised his voice in a shout. "Lucca, go aloft and take a look."

Castignoni picked up the little mechanism he used for remote control, and pushed a switch. The *Ripple* began gliding rapidly toward the playful porpoises. But now there were few birds overhead to indicate the presence of fish. The porpoises soon came to act as pilots, rolling and leaping beyond the curling foam of the cutwater.

"Nothing in sight," the mastman reported from above.

"Only about twenty tons from that big school," murmured Steve.

"Could be worse," observed the captain. And, lifting his voice again, he bellowed at the men below. "Start stowing the fish away, boys. That'll be all for a while."

Steve glanced at the clock, and seeing that it was almost noon, he went into the captain's room for the sextant. Randy followed him onto the wing, intending to go to the lower deck to help the men, but a call from the captain stopped him. "Show Randy how to use that, Steve."

Eight bells struck as Steve grasped the handle at the back of the brass instrument and peered through an eyehole. Making several slow adjustments of the center arm, he glanced at the graduated scale on the side and then handed the piece to Randy.

"A sextant gets its name because it's a sixth of a circle," Steve explained. "Look in the hole. Like a small telescope, isn't it? All you do is move the thing up or down until that hairline is at the meeting place of sky and water. Slowly adjust the arm then until the solar image is on the horizon line. The sun is reflected by tiny mirrors within, in case you're wondering. With the angle you obtain from the scale, you know your latitude and longitude—in other words, your position at sea."

Noticing Randy's puzzled expression, Steve grinned. "Come in," he said. "I'll show you."

They went to the chart table in the captain's room. Steve scratched figures on a pad, explaining each step. When he finished, he placed a dot on the chart and with a ruler continued the jagged line marking their passage southward from San Diego. From the end of the line he moved his pencil to the closest distinctive feature on the chart.

"Hmmmm. Point Abreojos should be northeast of us." Peering from the window, he indicated a prominent bluff rising against the stark brown mountains. "There she is. And a Mexican fishing boat is heading into Abreojos Anchorage east of it, giving us a double check. Now you do it."

Tearing the top sheet from the pad, he jotted down the figure taken from the sextant's scale, and passed over the pencil. Arithmetic had been Randy's best subject at school, but now, confused and nervous, he made several mistakes. His final figure differed from Steve's.

The navigator whistled, took the pencil and ran it along the chart to Randy's position. "Whew! We're coming into Mexico City!"

Randy flushed. "I did something wrong. Mind showing me again?"

Steve did. And by watching closely now, Randy duplicated the result with a second set of calculations. Then, at random, Steve gave him imaginary sextant readings to let him work out positions from them. He was slow, and at first made frequent errors, but before long he got accurate results.

"Like returning to school, isn't it? But you'll soon have it."

"I hope so," Randy said ruefully. "But I'd sure hate to sail with a fellow like me figuring the positions!"

The skipper called Randy to the wheel, and leaving Steve on watch, he went below. They followed a generally southward course in their continued search for tuna, but far from a straight one. Each time the mountains sank low into the sea to the eastward or the breakers were audible off to port, Steve ordered a turn.

Two schools of yellowfins and a smaller one of skipjacks were found, and each time the racks were lowered and Doc Bernedetto chummed to draw tuna to the boat. But none of the fish would take either squids or baited hooks. After each failure the captain would send Randy back to the wheel.

He was helmsman most of the next day as well. Twice during the morning and once early in the afternoon, traveling schools were located, but again the tuna refused all inducements. When the day was waning and most of the chums gone, the skipper ordered Steve to sail for Magdalena Bay while he lay down for a few hours rest.

Randy knew from his father's accounts that the bay toward which he was steering was one of the greatest baitfishing grounds on earth. Tuna fishermen venturing into tropical latitudes usually stopped there to take anchovettas. It was the northern range of these small fish, and they would remain active and healthy in a boat's tanks through long cruises in equatorial seas. Sardines and anchovies from the north, however, could be transported no farther south than Cape San Lucas, at the tip of the Lower California Peninsula. The brine being constantly pumped from the sea into the bait tanks would by then be too warm for them, whereas it was the natural element for anchovettas.

The boy thought of this as he stood on the duckboards. Now able to steer a reasonably straight course with little conscious attention, he watched the harsh outline of the mountains to the southeast. As the afterglow faded, their rugged contours were softened by shadows, then slowly dimmed with gathering haze, until only a silhouette remained, looming darkly against the star-bright sky. After a time the summits were touched with light, and somewhat later the moon rose, turning the sea to silver.

"Understand, I'm not beefing, Steve," Randy began abruptly, "but I've been wondering . . ."

Turning from the window, the navigator pushed up his visored cap, his teeth flashing in a quick smile. "You've been wondering whether the willing horse will continue to haul the biggest load, eh?" he asked, trying to guess the boy's question.

"No, it isn't that, exactly. I was thinking it was kind of funny that Louie never takes the wheel."

"He did, the men say, when he first sailed with his father."

"Couldn't he get the hang of it?"

"All the boys say he could, but wouldn't. He'd steer a corkscrew course each time he was at the helm, until the skipper gave up on him."

"You mean he deliberately steered a zigzag course?" Randy asked in amazement.

"It would seem so. Anyhow, something very similar happened one time when the captain left his oldest son behind in San Diego to study navigation and radio. Louie stuck one course for three days, the other for two. And when the Old Man went around later to talk to the instructors, they couldn't explain it. Louie was better than average, they claimed, and they didn't know why he'd quit."

"Too much work, maybe?"

Steve shook his head. "Louie's not lazy. Watch him hauling a seine or fishing or swabbing a deck. No one could put more into it. You find the answer, Randy. I can't!"

Off to the northeast, perhaps a quarter-mile away, a long spit had become visible. It ended in a domed hill, and beyond were several exposed rocks and a glowing line of breakers where a reef awaited unwary vessels. Steve gestured toward the hill.

"Entrada Point," he explained. "And across the entrance from it is our other landmark, Redondo Point, just coming into view. Redondo is at the western end of Santa Margarita Island; we'll be sailing along the eastern side to reach Almejas Bay."

On the island's bold headland a light had appeared. Randy dimly made out the masonry tower beneath it, a pale blur against the shadowy rise of Santa Margarita's impressive mountains.

"The entrance is wide enough," Steve said, walking over, "but the currents are tricky. Suppose I take her through."

Only a few minutes later the clipper was rocking and vibrating in the rips and whirlpools churning up the channel. The wheel twisted and jerked even in the navigator's strong hands. The entrance dropped behind, and they glided smoothly through the glassy ebony and silver swells of Magdalena Bay.

"Can't we get bait here?" Randy asked. For even by the

light of the moon and stars he could see that the magnificent bay they had entered stretched away to the north and for miles to the eastward as well, before meeting a barrier of bare hills.

Steve spun the wheel, and the *Ripple* swung southeastward. "The skipper has better luck in the adjoining body of water, Almejas Bay."

Off to starboard the mountains were rising higher against the starry sky, while the low, sandy hills were drawing nearer to the port side of the vessel. Then Magdalena was left behind, and the clipper slipped along a glistening waterway winding between the shores of island and mainland.

"Marcy Channel," observed Steve. "Takes us to Almejas. . . ."

Before he could finish Randy saw a submerged object, seemingly as large as their boat. It glowed with a phosphorescent radiance in the channel directly on their course.

"Rock dead ahead, Steve!" the boy bellowed.

"It couldn't be. . . ."

But then Steve saw whatever it was that lay beneath the surface. Without a moment's delay, he shoved the arrow of the ship's telegraph to reverse, then twisted the wheel hard over.

The *Ripple* shook violently, timbers creaking, agitated waters boiling astern. With more room for maneuvering, she might have responded in time to her rudder, might have come to a stop. But Randy saw his warning had come too late. Now, with a collision imminent, he grasped the brass grab-rail running beneath the windows. At least it might save him from being hurled against the opposite bulkhead.

"Brace yourself, Steve!" he called hoarsely. *"We're going to strike!"*

CHAPTER FIVE

A Manta Ray in the Seine

RANDY WAS so sure the clipper would be badly shaken upon striking the submerged object, that he was startled to feel only a slight vibration. The obstacle had vanished beneath the forepeak, except for a luminous fan of phosphorescence resembling the tail of a gigantic fish. But whereas a fish's tail was vertical, this glowing triangle of light spread horizontal beneath the water!

As it disappeared a peal of laughter burst from Steve Vardon.

"Wh-what's funny?" Randy faltered. "That rock might have sunk us!"

"The only shoals ahead, Randy, are at the other end of Marcy Channel. We grazed a sounding whale. They often feed in Almejas Bay."

Continuing on along the mile-wide channel, they swung starboard to avoid Horseshoe Shoals at the southern end, and entered a large bay. Randy judged it was approximately twelve miles long and two-thirds as wide. Moonlight softened the low rise of the mainland's hills, while across the platinum water to the right the soaring slopes of Santa Margarita Island had a silvery sheen. The anchor lights of several tuna boats glimmered off the island's eastern shore.

As they turned that way, Randy realized that the navigator had been right about the whale. Five of the great monsters were visible to the southeast. Another whale rose to blow at that moment, its enormous gray-black body shining wetly in the moonlight. Its spout billowed up like a fountain above the bright water, and a little later the boy heard the metallic whistling sound of its expelled breath.

"Let's not hit another whale, Steve!"

The navigator chuckled. "See if you can spot a school of anchovettas, Randy."

The boy stepped to a starboard window, but he could detect nothing in the water until they approached the first tuna boat. A ghostly blue radiance emanated from a pursed seine drawn up alongside the vessel. Fishermen were transferring chums to the bait tanks. The *Ripple* passed three other boats, and Randy saw that two of the craft had been lucky in finding anchovettas. Then, while they coasted along the shore of the island for a mile and more, the boy stared across the glistening bay without seeing anything.

Suddenly he noticed a patch of ruffled water not far off the beach, and when he had peered intently at it for a few moments he made out livid blue flashes playing along the surface.

"Could that be anything, Steve?" Randy asked, pointing.

After a short deliberation the navigator pushed the telegraph lever to *Slow,* muttering, "Hard to say when it's this bright."

The *Ripple* chugged along for several hundred yards. The peculiar electric-blue radiance of the water grew more pronounced, until Randy realized that it was caused by innumerable small fish stirring sparks of sea fire. Steve whistled, and brought the clipper drifting to a stop.

"No sense in scattering them," he said.

He jerked the signal cord several times. The clanging of the bell brought the boat to life. Sleepy voices drifted up from below, and presently feet pattered along deck. The giant Nicco Puccinelli and his little friend Ortorio appeared, pajama legs flapping as they dashed forward to let go the anchor. The chain was still rattling and clanking when Captain Castignoni stepped onto the bridge. Soberly he peered at the stretch of luminous blue water, and then turned back to his room to dress.

No time was lost in launching the boats. Only a little over a half-hour after the clipper came to anchor, Steve was at the wheel of the speedboat, towing the two skiffs toward the southward-moving school of fish. The smaller skiff was released as before to help drag the seine from the net-skiff. And when the latter boat had been pulled on a circular course by the launch, the webbing held thousands of fish that streaked the water in their darting efforts to escape.

Doc Bernedetto made a swift grab and held up a wriggling fish in the moonlight. "Anchovettas," he declared. "But we're losing them!"

It was true! At the opposite side of the net there was a rippling silver flow over the submerged cork-line. Steve quickly towed the smaller skiff around to the low side to support the seine.

Tony Riggio slipped into the light diving gear and descended to purse the bottom of the net and tie it securely.

With this done, the heavily laden seine was hauled alongside the *Ripple*, and the scooping of anchovettas into the bait tanks began.

The transfer of these chums and those from a second set of the net was made without mishap. But when the speedboat was towing the purse seine and the two skiffs back to the boat the third time, disaster struck without the slightest warning.

A sudden stress on the webbing tilted the net skiff over so sharply that brine flowed over the gunwale. Every man in the boat save one managed to grasp a thwart, to avoid being flung overboard. It was Nicco Puccinelli's misfortune to be standing. His huge body made a splash that drenched the others. Randy and Riggio quickly dragged their giant mate into the boat. Puccinelli sat quietly in his dripping clothes for a moment, and then a startled expression came over his large childlike face. Springing up with a yell, he jumped about in such a frenzy that the skiff rocked and creaked. Riggio reached for an oar to subdue him, believing that the huge man had lost his mind. Puccinelli stopped jigging, however, when two anchovettas slipped from the leg of his dungarees.

"They tickled," he grunted. "I bet we caught a whale!"

The men leaned on the gunwale to see if he was right. It was well they did! For at that moment another violent wrench on the net whipped the boat over like a child's toy. The standing men were catapulted through the air; not one was struck by the boat when it overturned.

Randy flew across the water and landed flat in a "bellyflop" that temporarily stunned him. He was annoyed, for he imagined that one of his mates had playfully pushed him overboard.

At the sound of splashing he turned and was surprised to see that his mates were also swimming. The boat had been dragged so far under that only its keel was visible. And not a single one of the cork floats supporting the seine was to be seen. Anchovettas, entrapped moments before, swam in all directions over the submerged cork-float line in obvious fright.

Steve Vardon had stopped the speedboat with the first pull on the net. Now, shouting at Ortorio to cast off the towline, he started turning the launch to come to their assistance.

Still puzzled as to what had caused the disturbance, Tony Riggio dropped his face into the water to look down. Randy filled his lungs with air and did likewise.

At first he saw nothing through the pale-green water except milling anchovettas and shimmering specks of sediment caught in the rays of the rising sun. Presently, beneath the cross-thatch of the net, he detected a shadowy, batlike form rising from the depths. The creature's pectoral fins, extending perhaps twenty feet between the tips, beat the water like enormous wings. The free forward ends of these wings, projecting beyond the head, were rolled up in a way that made them resemble horns.

It was these horns that enabled Randy to identify the monster. It was a great devilfish, or manta ray! Ordinarily quite harmless giants, these enormous rays could go into a flurry of destruction if restrained. They had been known to tangle themselves in anchor chains, snap the chains and then tow boats for hours before becoming exhausted. And, often enough, they turned on the boats thus captured, trying to smash them with their powerful wings.

Randy realized, with a twinge of alarm, that this great devilfish had become enmeshed in their seine; its struggles to break away had submerged the cork-float line and capsized their skiffs.

He started at a fast crawl toward the speedboat. Ortorio was helping Riggio over the side. The two of them then dragged the other dripping men into the cockpit. No sooner was Randy aboard than Steve opened the throttle, and the power-boat roared toward the smaller skiff. Though it had reappeared after being pulled entirely beneath the surface, Doc Bernedetto and the cook were swimming toward the *Ripple*. Steve glided up beside the two men and they were taken into the boat.

The moment they were rescued, Steve sped toward the clipper. There was ample reason for haste. Both the cork-float line and the skiffs had once more disappeared. Seething currents showed that the manta ray was engaged in a herculean struggle to free itself of the seine. Before the speedboat reached the ship, the skiff and the line bobbed up. Short fragments of webbing were attached to the line, indicating that the larger portion of the net had been torn away.

Now, for the first time, the giant ray appeared, lashing the water into clouds of vapor in its efforts to break the entangling strands of cording still clinging to its wings and head. Burdened by the seine's weight, however, the monster could not long remain on the surface. It sank from sight, whirlpools swirling in its wake.

Minutes passed before it reappeared. The bay foamed and bubbled as the ray's mighty wings smashed the surface with blows that clapped like rifle shots. Spray rose in iridescent mists. And though this infuriated turmoil continued for the space of several long breaths, a few cords of the seine were wrapped around one pectoral fin when the manta once more vanished.

Somewhere in the depths the monster ripped away these cords. For when it rose again, several hundred yards to the northeast, it was no longer entangled in the net. It sped away, its body submerged save for batlike wings that rose and fell against the sunlit water.

"*Whew!*" Steve cried hoarsely. "I'm glad it didn't come this way!"

"We've got to mark the place where the net sank!" Riggio said anxiously. "We don't have a spare one."

The wisdom of this was evident. The anchovettas already transferred to the bait tanks would not last many days. And without a seine, it would be impossible to take more.

Steve headed out to the net skiff. A line was put on a thwart and after two failures, the men righted it and its original crew returned to their places. The speedboat then towed it to the spot where the net had last been seen. The navigator had to return to the clipper for a hook and a line suitable for dragging. While he was gone Riggio fashioned a marker buoy by tying one end of a hundred-foot line to an empty oil can and the other to the skiff's small anchor. Only twenty feet of the rope remained when the anchor touched bottom.

"Our seine's eighty feet down!" Riggio said with a groan. "You'd need a complete diving dress to go that deep. Dragging is our only hope."

Steve soon returned with a hook and rope. Ortorio, holding this dragline, was almost pulled from the speedboat when the hook caught on something heavy. The navigator shifted into neutral and walked aft to help. With great difficulty, he and Ortorio hauled aboard a huge mass of kelp. They tried twice more, but with the same result.

"It's hopeless to drag in this kelp," Steve decided. "Tony will have to go down with the aqua-lung."

Riggio's dark eyes flashed. "Do I look that crazy, eh? Do I?"

"Sure," said Steve good naturedly. "If I weren't such a poor swimmer, I'd try it. . . . Let's see what Joe says."

Leaving the bobbing oil can to mark the location, Steve towed the net skiff back to the *Ripple*. He left it there, and skimmed away to recover the smaller skiff. He brought it in with the cork line trailing astern.

Captain Castignoni had meanwhile been trying, without success, to persuade Riggio to give the new diving equipment a trial.

"You'll never talk Tony into trying anything new, Joe," said Steve. "I'll see if any boat in the bay has an extra seine."

The skipper watched the speedboat glide away, and shook his head. "Not many boats carry two nets," he said. "We've either got to use the aqua-lung to recover our seine, or lose considerable time sailing to some port where we can buy another."

"Don't look at me!" snapped Tony Riggio. "I won't go down in any self-contained gear! I want a lifeline handy so I can be pulled up if anything goes wrong."

Castignoni said brusquely, "Who is willing to try it?" When no one spoke, he added, "Frank would if he were here. How about you, Louie?"

Louie grimaced. "No thanks! I want to stay alive!"

The captain's mention of his younger son started a chain reaction in Randy. He knew Joe Castignoni was right: the novelty of the aqua-lung would have strongly appealed to Frank's venturesome nature. Randy would have been tempted to try it, too, had not Riggio cast doubts on the safety of the device. Thoughts of Frank awakened another memory in Randy's mind. He recalled the captain's gruff warning that he would expect as much of Randy as of his younger son.

A feeling of shame swept over the boy as the captain swung around and started toward his cabin, saying, "I've never asked a man to do anything I won't do myself. I'll dive for that seine!"

Though thoroughly frightened by the prospect, Randy blurted, "I—I'd like to try it first, sir."

Joe Castignoni wheeled, an expression of surprise in his brown, hawklike face. "Very well," he said briskly. "Get into your trunks. I'll slip on mine, too. Riggio and I can help if you need us."

Randy felt somewhat relieved as he hurried to his cabin. He knew that both Riggio and the captain were remarkably good swimmers.

When he came aft a short time later, he saw that the aqua-lung equipment had been stowed in the net skiff. Louie, Riggio and Puccinelli were waiting there, and the captain soon joined them.

"Head inshore, Nicco," the captain said as Puccinelli picked up the oars. "We'll let Randy try diving in shallow water first."

The big fisherman rowed until the skiff was but half a dozen yards beyond the light line of breakers rolling in to-ward the beach of Santa Margarita Island. Riggio, who was still in bathing trunks, slipped over the gunwale, allowed himself to sink to the bottom, and then bobbed up and clambered over the side.

"About ten feet deep," he said. "All right, Randy?"

"F-fine," said the boy.

Riggio immediately started to help Randy into his diving rig. Because the boy had a large frame, the hardest part was to pull on the skin-tight suit of yellow-brown gum rubber, for he had to slide in through an opening in the back that was later tied securely. The dress completely enveloped him except for an oval space around his face. And a harness, pass-ing over his shoulders and buckling across his chest, held a cylinder of compressed air on his back. Two flexible rubber tubes of large diameter—like those used in gas masks, though capable of withstanding greater pressure—ran around either side of his head from the air-tank to a rub-ber bit he gripped in his teeth. Two holes, set at opposite sides of the bit, brought in air from one hose and passed his exhaled breath out the other to a respirator attached to the cylinder. A round plate of shatterproof glass, covering Randy's eyes and nose, was snapped in place with a rubber band encircling his head. And on his feet went large swim fins of French design. When finally dressed, the boy looked like fanciful illustrations of the space men of science fiction.

Apparently the captain knew little more about the equipment than Randy, for while the boy was being helped into the rig, Joe Castignoni read the instructions and explained them in his own words.

"You have a forty-minute air supply, Randy. But don't swim too fast or you'll breathe deeply and exhaust your air more quickly. . . . If your ears ache, don't descend any farther until they are unblocked. Swim at that level while blowing and swallowing. When your ears pop, the pressure inside and outside your head will once more be equalized."

Randy had been holding the rubber bit loosely, in order to breathe through his mouth. Now Riggio turned the valve of the aqua-lung, and a jet of warm air hissed into the boy's mouth, making his tongue and throat feel uncomfortably dry. He clamped his teeth on the bit, grasped the skiff's gunwale, and slid over the side into the water.

Although he allowed himself to sink until his feet touched bottom, he was so shaken with panic then that he kicked hard to bob up to the surface. Snatching off the face mask, he breathed deeply.

"Anything wrong?" Captain Castignoni shouted anxiously.

Ashamed of his alarm, Randy shook his head. He pulled

on his vision plate once more, and sank through the pale-green water. The air tank, which had seemed so cumbersome and heavy before, appeared to weigh almost nothing in the sea. And his lung fed a steady jet of air into his mouth. Yet so great was the boy's mistrust of the strange device that after a dozen strokes, he gave several frantic kicks to bring himself up.

Again, Randy immediately felt ashamed of his fear. Before the captain could speak, he dived and swam for a few strokes under water. But the same sensation of impending disaster washed over him. Kicking and sculling wildly, he drove himself to the surface and swam toward the boat. Not until he gripped the gunwale did his alarm subside.

Captain Castignoni was plainly annoyed. "If you're afraid of this gear, Randy," he shouted, "let me try it."

Randy already regretted the impulse that had led him to volunteer as a deep-sea diver. But the dogged quality that always made him reluctant to give up anything undertaken now stiffened his determination.

He pulled out his mouthpiece and said, "Give me a few minutes to get accustomed to the aqua-lung, sir. It—it seems to work all right, but I'm not used to swimming with so much gear."

"All right," said the captain gruffly.

While being dressed, Randy had watched Steve Vardon skimming from one tuna boat to another. But the speedboat had lingered such a short time alongside each clipper that Steve was obviously having no success in finding a spare seine. Now the launch was in pursuit of a boat sailing southward toward the *Ripple*.

If he could locate a net, Randy thought, *I wouldn't have to find the one we lost.*

Believing there was small chance of that, however, Randy made three more dives, remaining below a little longer each time. The lung operated perfectly. But in spite of that, Riggio's distrust had so shaken the boy's confidence in the strange diving gear that he felt uneasy every moment he was below.

Feeling discouraged after his last dive, Randy swam to the boat and removed his face plate and mouthpiece. He was on the verge of asking the captain to relieve him when he noticed that the tuna clipper sailing southward had now stopped. The *Ripple's* speedboat lay alongside, and at that moment a fisherman dropped into the cockpit beside Steve. The boat started with a roar, and as it was pounding toward the net skiff, Randy decided to wait to see what this might mean before speaking to the captain.

Presently Steve shut off the motor and glided up to the skiff. Standing beside him and Ortorio was a youth of medium stature, with bare, muscular brown arms. Not until a grin lighted the newcomer's broad face and chocolate-colored eyes, however, did Randy recognize his basketball teammate, Hal Lassman. Twelve months before, upon his graduation from high school, Hal had become a tuna fisherman, and in that time tropical sunlight had burned him to a mahogany hue.

"I couldn't find a spare net," Steve said. "But Lassman here knows something about aqua-lungs."

"I'm the *Victory Belle's* diver," Hal explained. "Every time we're in port I go up to a sporting-goods store to ask questions about lungs. I'm trying to persuade the skipper to buy one. . . . Swim over here, Randy, and let's see if you're rigged up right."

Randy was only too glad to do so, for he had serious doubts about that. Hal examined every part of the device with care.

"Looks all right," he said at length. "Does it give any trouble?"

"N-no," the boy faltered. "But I'm afraid my air will shut off."

"That can't happen with this gear," Hal reassured him. "The Costeau-Gagnon valve regulates your air supply at any depth. Providing," Hal added with a grin, "you don't descend more than the 228 feet reached by the French diver Frederick Dumas with one of these lungs. Did you notice the respirator on your tank?"

"The gadget that looks like a large microphone?"

"That's it, Randy. In that respirator is a sensitive air-demand valve. Your exhaled breath exerts pressure on that valve, regulating it to feed you air from the tank in exactly the quantity you expel. As you go deeper the pressure on your body increases, you exhale with greater force, and thereby release a larger amount of air. Thus you're always breathing air at the pressure of the surrounding water."

"How will I know whether my tank is running low, Hal?"

"Easy, boy! One-eighth of the air in your cylinder is an emergency supply. When you're down to that point, your air line constricts and you'll find it hard to breathe. Then simply reach back and flip the lever on your tank to release your emergency supply, and come up."

After Randy had asked several other questions, Hal said, "Let's see you swim around the boat."

Randy slipped his mouthpiece and mask in place, and with sculling motions of his hands propelled himself toward the bottom. Now, understanding how his equipment worked, he was no longer afraid his air supply might fail.

Moving his arms with long, easy strokes and kicking steadily with his swim fins, he glided through passages between the larger boulders. In drawing near rocks studded with barnacles, purple sea-urchins and shellfish that would scratch his knees and legs, he made downward motions with his cupped palms to pass over them. Strands of kelp did not impede his progress, for he slipped through them like a fish, pressing aside the olive-brown blades and stalks with hands and body. And when he peered below him, he could see the surface swells playing across the bottom rocks, the whorled shells of gastropods and hermit crabs, and the luxurious gold and ruby and violet and rainbow-tinted marine plants attached to every ledge and boulder.

Best of all, Randy was discovering that the unique air-demand valve of the aqua-lung allowed him to remain in static balance with small effort on his part. Little strength was required to remain submerged, to force himself to greater depth, or to ascend. Hal Lassman had banished the boy's doubts about the safety of the device. And now, enjoying the freedom of movement it gave him in an alien world,

Randy completed a second circuit of the boats before coming up.

"You're a fair swimmer," Hal said as Randy removed his mask.

Captain Castignoni reached over to grasp Randy's hand and help him into the skiff. "Let's try to find the net," he said.

A line was made fast to the skiff, and Steve towed it out to the oil-can buoy. Since it would no longer be needed to mark the spot, the navigator hauled the can aboard and heaved up the anchor. He untied the wet line and cast it to Randy.

"Secure this to the seine if you can find it, Randy."

As the boy started to coil the rope loosely about his body, Hal said, "If you're uneasy about that aqua-lung, I'll hunt for the net."

Randy sensed that Hal Lassman was eager to try the equipment himself. It was important, however, that at least one man on the *Ripple* know how to use the lung. And having started his apprenticeship, the boy decided he might as well continue.

"Let me see what I can do first, Hal," he said.

He slid over the side of the skiff and clung to the gunwale with one hand while he adjusted his face plate and mouthpiece.

"Don't come up too fast!" Hal shouted. "If you do, you might get the bends."

The warning had a sobering effect on Randy, for it recalled accounts of California abalone divers who had suffered bends from being pulled up too quickly by their line-tenders. In breathing compressed air, they had absorbed abnormal amounts of oxygen and nitrogen, and their sudden ascents had not allowed time for the excess nitrogen to be released from their lungs. The sluggish gas had frothed into bubbles in their blood exactly as bubbles are released upon the opening of a bottle of soda pop. If these bubbles lodged in the joints, the heart or the brain, the diver was either paralyzed or died.

It was not a pleasant reminder to a boy about to make his first deep descent with a strange diving device!

CHAPTER SIX

Blue Depths with the

Aqua-Lung

RANDY STARTED his dive, sculling with his hands, kicking with his feet to drive himself down. He swam on a wide, spiralling course as he descended, hoping thereby to reach bottom somewhere near the lost purse-seine.

Nothing at first appeared before his vision plate save specks of sediment, shimmering brilliantly in the clear emerald water. But presently he saw a small group of anchovettas that scattered like a shower of tinsel at his approach. Propelling himself steadily downward, he glided past long, weaving streamers of kelp. Fish hidden in the purple shadows cast by the kelp blazed with bluish or silvery fire when caught in vagrant gleams of sunlight. Small squids, trailing their translucent bodies like tiny, collapsed parachutes, expelled jets of water to dart away from the strange visitor streaming bubbles in his wake.

Feeling pain mounting in his ears and behind his eyes, Randy recalled the instructions Captain Castignoni had read. His aural passages must be blocked! He must open them before he blacked out! Bringing himself to a horizontal position and swimming slowly, he blew against his tightly closed lips and swallowed repeatedly. The probing pressure grew almost unbearable, but instantly vanished when his ears popped. Randy resumed his slow, spiralling descent.

Gradually the water lost its greenish hue and became more and more blue until it had the soft, glowing radiance of light filtering through a stained-glass window. This weird illumination gave everything passing before his face plate an atmosphere of fantasy, of unreality that he had known before only in dreams. Fish gliding through the swaying stalks of kelp, lacy sea-plants undulating in the currents, the tumbled wilderness of gigantic rocks and broken ledges presently visible below him were all blue. And winding through the chaos of boulders was what appeared to be a river, pale sapphire in color, glowing with the electric quality of a marine grotto. But this, too, was part of the fantasy. For as he dove himself deeper, the submarine waterway became a canyon, where the sea floor had been torn asunder in some past volcanic upheaval.

Once again sharp stabs of pain warned Randy that the pressure of the water bearing on him from all sides was greater than the air pressure in his inner ear. He had to blow and swallow numerous times before the unblocking of his aural passages was announced by an explosive *crack*. The sudden relief made his senses momentarily spin, but the feeling of faintness quickly vanished when he kicked to elevate his feet and bring the blood to his head.

As his vision cleared, he found himself staring down into the deep crevasse. Clearly he could make out masses of marine plants and animals, crowded for living space on the upper walls, but the bottom recesses were lost in blue mists. Somewhere down there, he thought, their seine might be resting. A little uneasily, he gave several flutter kicks with his fins to venture downward into the undersea canyon. Instantly he felt the flowing thrust of a strong current.

Unexpected as this was, it was the sensation of entrapment caused by the narrowing sides rather than the current that made him take desperate strokes to escape. The walls glided swiftly past, and in a moment he was swimming once more above the winding blue river.

He was breathing too much air because of the scare, and now he barely moved arms and legs while he fought for composure. Fright, he suspected, might well lead him into doing something foolish.

When he could breathe normally again, he began moving in a slow spiral through the swaying draperies of kelp. His eyes roved in a ceaseless search for the net. The bottom was unbelievably rough; beneath a tangle of sea growth he could detect the outlines of rocks pitched at every angle. In places the stalks and blades of kelp formed seemingly impenetrable barriers to his progress, but he discovered that he could press them aside to make slow, if difficult, headway. The thick kelp limited his vision to a few yards, however, and he was uncomfortably aware that he might pass the seine without seeing it.

When he saw the crevasse again, he made a second and wider circle, and then a third. Fighting back his nervousness then, he descended into the deep gorge in the sea floor. The current, while strong, was no match for his swim-fins, and he could force his way against it by kicking steadily. The angling contours of the submarine canyon led him on and on, until he became convinced that the net could not lie on its bottom.

Randy turned then, and, stroking lightly, allowed the swift current to carry him back between the rock walls to his starting point. The steep rock sides were an ever-changing panorama of marine life: great purple sea-urchins, weaving long, needle-sharp spines; ear-shaped abalones of a species he had never seen; enormous sea-anemones, weaving their tentacles in search of food; crabs and rock lobsters prowling through elfin forests of sea plants.

When at length he emerged from the crevasse, Randy was finding it difficult to obtain enough air. Not at first suspecting the real reason, he tried blowing and swallowing. But the tightness about his chest only grew more pronounced, as though he were being squeezed by water pressure. Panic started to grip him. Then he recalled Hal Lassman's explanation about the aqua-lung's emergency air supply. Randy could not believe he had been below long enough to use seven-eighths of his air, but when he reached back and pulled the lever on his tank, a strong jet of air once more flowed into his mouth and he could breathe freely. With but an eighth of his air supply remaining, however, he must start his ascent!

Randy took his time about this. He swam in slow spirals, pausing frequently to blow and swallow and to exercise vigorously. The exercise, he hoped, might expel much of the dangerous nitrogen from his blood. A silver sheet at last slipped past his vision plate, and he was in the sunlight again, though many yards from the boats. He swam slowly to the skiff and was helped into it. And he was so tired that after his equipment was removed, he flopped down in the bottom of the boat, where he lay gasping for breath.

"Do you feel all right, Randy?" the skipper asked anxiously.

"Y-yes, sir. But trying to—find the seine down there—it's like looking for a cat's hair in a haystack."

Hal Lassman pulled the boats together with the towline and stepped into the skiff. He examined the aqua-lung for a few minutes, and then smiled up at Joe Castignoni.

"I'd like to have a try at it, Captain, if you have a spare tank."

"We have nine," said the skipper, and he turned to the navigator. "Steve, bring one over. You'll find them in the net locker."

Ortorio cast off the line. Steve Vardon sped over to the tuna boat and climbed aboard.

A chill torpor had crept into Randy's blood in the depths, but the hot sun beating upon his back soon had him feeling warm and relaxed. He sat up and stretched.

"Why aren't you sailing on your dad's boat?" Hal asked.

"Dad's boat is too small to sail this far south, and I'm trying to find Frank Castignoni."

Hal sobered. "Last cruise I saw him right here in Almejas Bay."

"Was the *Westwind* on her way north or south?" Randy asked tersely.

"Southward, I'm sorry to say."

"Had she had any engine trouble on her way down here, Hal?"

Hal shook his head. "I had a chance to talk to Frank when we were both out bait fishing. He said the *Westwind* had never made as fast a run to Magdalena Bay."

Still hoping to uncover some clue to the clipper's disappearance, Randy asked, "Did she take on much bait here?"

"Yes. She filled all three bait tanks and two bait-wells with chums. She had enough anchovettas to fish all the way to Panama, or even as far south as Peru. That's a considerable amount of ocean, so her bait supply isn't much help in determining where she disappeared."

"No," Randy said with disappointment.

After a long pause Hal said, "An odd thing happened while we were here, Randy. Our boat and another clipper refueled from extra Diesel oil we'd brought along. It would have taken too long to hold the thirty oil drums we'd emptied under water until they filled and sank; and if we'd left them floating in the bay, any boat striking one of them might have stove in her bow. So the drums were taken ashore in net skiffs and lined up beyond highwater mark, in case some Mexican might want them for a stove or boiler. No sooner had our skiffs returned than Captain Vittorio Castignoni sent out his boats to haul the barrels back to the *Westwind*."

Even after having heard Steve Vardon's accounts of Vittorio Castignoni's activities as a marine junkman, the story surprised Randy. "What did he do with the drums, Hal?"

"Stowed them below deck, I suppose."

"My brother was always doing things like that," said Joe

Castignoni thoughtfully. "He planned to collect the three-fifty refund from the oil company when he got back, I suppose."

Before Randy could decide whether the thirty empty oil drums might provide a clue to the mystery, the speedboat drew alongside and stopped. Ortorio passed the fresh air tank to Riggio. The bald-headed little man had soon dressed Hal Lassman in the diving outfit.

Hal made several short, preliminary dives to accustom himself to the aqua-lung. Then, kicking vigorously, he started his descent. His air-bubbles rose in a milky-green boil, which became small eruptions whenever he blew harder to clear a blockage in his ears. Only nine minutes after Hal had disappeared, Randy saw his friend far below the boat. Moments later Hal bobbed up and was helped aboard.

"Lung works—great," he gasped, as soon as he could speak. "But it's like—a mangrove thicket down there— *Kelp!*"

"Guess we'll have to give up," said the skipper. "We can sail around Cape San Lucas and try to find a seine at La Paz."

"Are we looking in the right place?" inquired Randy. "It's true we last sighted the seine about here. But I'm wondering if I tried again, closer to the spot where the manta came up the final time, if I wouldn't be nearer the location where the net was actually shaken off."

The captain deliberated. "Sure you're not too tired, Randy?"

"No, sir. Not now."

Steve towed the skiff, as nearly as he could recollect, to the point where he believed the manta had broken water after its last dive. As soon as Randy was once more in his equipment, he slipped over the side of the boat and started downward.

The first sixty feet of his descent was little different than his previous one, but at that point his way was obstructed by something that wrapped itself around him, bringing him to a slow halt. Believing that it was unusually dense kelp, Randy tried to forge through it by hard kicks of his swimfins, only to find himself becoming more hopelessly enmeshed. Alarmed at the thought that he was being trapped far from the surface, he lashed out with hands and feet in a desperate effort to escape. He was brought to his senses by the realization that he was breathing too fast and exhaling at a rate that would exhaust his air much more quickly than usual. Hal Lassman had depleted the supply in the tank. Randy knew he must conserve what was left.

Worming his arm through the masses of kelp entwined about his body, he carefully disengaged the tangled strands. His hand touched something that felt like a wet, hard fiber, entirely lacking the slippery surface of a kelp stalk or blade. Randy pulled himself into an erect position to see more clearly. He was startled to find himself peering through what seemed to be a shadowy spider-web outlined against the misty-blue glow of the sea. His first frightened thought was that he had blundered into a web constructed by some spider-like monster of the deeps to capture its prey.

Quickly he abandoned that absurd notion. No such trap

could withstand the action of tides and swells. What he had discovered was the *Ripple's* seine! But why had it failed to reach the bottom?

In a moment Randy guessed the reason. After being cast off by the manta, the net had carried down masses of kelp in its descent, until so many of these sea plants were caught in the folds of webbing that their air-bladders had prevented the seine from sinking deeper.

Randy knew he must work back slowly through the tangled stalks and blades to avoid dislodging the net from the kelp supporting it. He did not breathe freely again until he had reached the edge of the seine. Then he tread water lightly, to hold his position while he unwound the line from his body and wove it through the cording for several yards before tying a knot.

His ascent was an ordeal, for the rope became entangled with kelp as he rose, making swimming difficult. He was almost exhausted when he came up beside the net skiff, and handed the line to Riggio.

"You found the seine?" the captain asked eagerly, as Randy was helped into the boat.

Randy pulled out the mouthpiece, pushed up the face plate, and dropped wearily onto a thwart. "Yes, sir. I made it fast."

When the men pulled up the net, however, it was found to be ripped and torn in scores of places.

"This seine will never hold another chum!" wailed Louie Castignoni.

"We can repair it," declared his father. "But it will be a

tough job."

Replacing the broken cording, as it turned out, required the work of every man aboard for the next two days. When the seine could once more be used for fishing, however, neither the *Ripple* nor any other boat could find bait. Anchovettas would unaccountably vanish from both Almejas and adjoining Magdalena bays at certain times, and on this occasion ten days were to pass before they reappeared.

One night shortly after recovering the net, Randy received permission to call his mother on the marine radiophone in the captain's cabin. His mother sounded happy to hear his voice, and after they had talked for several minutes she said, "There's someone here who'd like to speak to you, Randy."

The boy's heart leapt as he recognized his father's voice. "How are you, Son?"

"Fine, Dad!" Randy exclaimed. "When did you get in?"

"Early yesterday morning. And we couldn't have stowed another tuna in our wells. Have you uncovered any clue to the *Westwind?*"

"No, Dad. No fresh ones."

"Well, keep at it, Randy. My own theory is that she was exploring new fishing grounds when something happened."

Randy repeated his father's words to the captain after he hung up, but Joe Castignoni made no comment.

Late one evening, following a long trick at the wheel, Randy left the bridge and climbed the rigging to visit with the mastman. He talked with Jack Lucca as the clipper sailed in slow zigzags across darkened Almejas Bay. Suddenly a glowing streak of silver caught Randy's attention, and he gripped his friend's arm.

"Anchovettas!" cried Lucca. "They've returned at last!"

Small boats were soon launched. Before the speedboat could take the skiffs in tow, the skipper appeared with the aqua-lung equipment and passed it down to Randy.

"You'll purse the seine," he said gruffly.

The captain's tone implied that he was still annoyed with Riggio for his refusal to use the lung. Though Joe Castignoni was never to mention the subject again, it was understood by everyone aboard that Randy had become the *Ripple's* diver.

When the first set of the net was made and Riggio began helping the boy into his diving gear, Randy was embarrassed.

"I don't like to take your job, Riggio," he said.

Riggio shrugged. "I don't get paid extra for diving. If you have any trouble, I'll come down and give you a hand."

Randy had no difficulty because every strand was brilliantly outlined with phosphorescence. It took him more time than usual, however, to descend, draw the bottom of the net together and tie it. The aqua-lung nevertheless gave him such freedom of movement that after a few dives he could purse the seine far more quickly than Riggio.

Anchovettas had appeared in the bay in such vast numbers that by morning thousands of small fish were swimming in endless circles in the *Ripple's* three bait-tanks and the two bait wells. Doc Bernedetto declared that no more could be taken without overcrowding.

The skiffs and speedboat were immediately taken aboard, and the clipper sailed through Marcy Channel and the entrance of Magdalena Bay into the open Pacific. Although everyone except the men on the bridge and engine-room watch had turned in without breakfast to recover from the hard work of hauling the seine, Randy lingered for a while at the rail to observe the ocean in one of its sullen moods. The rolling hills of water had a metallic glitter, fast fading to a somber gray as a heavy overcast spread across the remaining patches of blue sky.

In early afternoon, when it became too hazardous to remain longer on automatic pilot, Randy was called to take the wheel. The boat was pitching and wallowing off the southern extremity of Lower California by then. Several hours later Steve Vardon pointed out two great, grotesque rocks, white with bird guano, which marked Cape San Lucas. It lay at the tip of the long peninsula, and beyond the cape was the broad entrance of the Gulf of California.

When the clipper lost the shelter of the coastal mountains, the gulf wind struck with fury, making her roll and pitch like a seagoing tugboat. Randy tried to let the vessel ride with the seas, but he was not always successful. Sometimes a surging swell caught her broadside, and the boat would tremble violently from the impact.

The captain emerged from his room, his dark face stern with anger. After a glance at the sea, however, he made no comment on how the boy was handling the wheel, but merely said quietly, "Better go down to mess now, Randy. You, too,

Steve. We're in for a bad night."

There was little conversation at the evening meal. And when the dishes were cleared away, all the men except Steve Vardon remained at the table, listening to the rising wind buffeting the clipper with hard blasts. Before long there was a continuous, shrieking wail that not even the closed door could exclude. The boat both rolled and pitched. Objects banged and clattered on all parts of the vessel. Randy could hear the swishing and seething of oil and brine in tanks and wells.

Julio Ortorio stroked his long, white mustache thoughtfully. "A *chubasco* is making, my friends," he said gravely.

Freshwater nodded soberly.

Randy felt a chill of uneasiness. He had heard of the tropical hurricanes off the Mexican coast. *Chubascos* disabled and sometimes sank tuna boats. While the *Ripple* crossed the broad throat of the gulf, she would have no land to shelter her from the fierce sweep of the wind. Nor was there any nearby port to which she could flee.

Suddenly the steady throbbing of the engines ceased. The clipper began to wallow, creaking and groaning as she heeled far starboard, and then, sluggishly recovering, started a long port roll. Puccinelli sprang up and dashed to the door, opening it just in time to be drenched by a sea breaking with a crash on the port side.

Gasping from the shock of the cold water, the big fisherman drew the door closed. "Our fuel pump must have broken down again," he declared.

"But, of course," said Ortorio. "Who would not know it?"

"We'll break up mighty quick," observed Jack Lucca nervously, "if the Chief doesn't fix it in a hurry."

An intercommunication speaker secured to the bulkhead began to buzz. The captain's voice, strangely altered, filled the room with sound: "Send Randy to the bridge."

Randy rose, and then felt a tremor in his knees as another sea crashed thunderously against the door. He could hear the seething hiss of water sweeping along the deck.

"Joe must be mad!" cried Ortorio. "Do not do this, Randy!"

But the boy, remembering his promise to the captain, took one stiff step after another, passing the stupefied Puccinelli and reaching out, with a hand that had suddenly become numb, for the doorknob. His eyes were blurred and he groped for it blindly. He was half-convinced that the moment he stepped on deck he'd be washed overboard.

"Wait, Randy!" shouted a hoarse voice, and the boy turned to see Freshwater striding toward him. "The skipper wouldn't ask anyone to go up on the bridge without a line when it's like this. Let me get it."

The big, freckled-faced fisherman grasped the knob and cautiously opened the door. The screeching wind drove salt spray into their faces. But the galley lights cast a faint glow upon a rope rippling in the deck wash. Freshwater made a grab for it, and would have been flung across the deck by the port roll of the vessel if Randy had not caught the man's belt.

He pulled Freshwater into the galley, and the big fisherman drew the door closed. But there was a crack caused by the line, and when a crashing sea pounded the panel, water

· 121 ·

streamed through this opening to drench Freshwater. Quite undismayed, he waited a few moments and then hurled back the door.

"Get a good grip on this line, Randy—I'll keep it taut," he cried. "The packet's starting a starboard roll. You can make it!"

Randy stepped out on deck. The swift wash, tugging at his ankles, would have upset him but for his grip on the rope. He splashed forward as fast as he could move, knowing that he must reach the bridge before the next port roll allowed the seas to come crashing over the rail once more. By the faint radiance of the riding light on the mast, he saw that the navigator's blond head was thrust from the wheelhouse door. Steve held the line taut and seemed to be urging him to greater speed, though Randy could not catch a word he was saying because of the thunderous clashing of the seas.

The *Ripple* was rolling to port when the boy at length scrambled up the ladder. Steve grasped his hand and pulled him inside.

Blue light from the gyro-compass showed Randy the strain in Captain Castignoni's forceful face. The skipper was spinning the wheel first one way, then the other, in an effort to control the vessel by rudder alone.

"Chance for you to learn what you're in for with a dead engine," Joe Castignoni said without turning. "Stand over here and watch me."

Randy walked to the captain's side. From the windows, he had an appalling view of the seas. They loomed above the wheelhouse, great hills of water tipped with flashing phosphorescence. In their power for destruction, they made the clipper appear like an insignificant toy as she dropped away into the troughs.

It seemed as if the boat would be crushed between the white-fanged jaws of water reaching ever for her. But they failed to catch her broadside—the captain saw to that. Still, the vessel was twisted and wrenched, for Joe Castignoni had but meager control. He brought the clipper up time and again, shaking and creaking, riding the enormous swells as they mounted, then lost momentum. The boat would at once plunge into the trough again. Walls of water would rush upward. It was a terrifying experience to Randy. He wondered how long the skipper could control the *Ripple* sufficiently to prevent her from being broken up in the seas.

The same thought must have been in Steve Vardon's mind, for he called, "Chief," into the engine-room speaking tube from time to time, but without at first receiving any reply.

Suddenly the anxiety left his face. "Mac says he's got the fuel pump working again!"

"Bless our crusty old chief!" cried the skipper with feeling.

Steve shoved the engine-room telegraph to *Slow*.

There was a low rumbling. The clipper began to tremble as her screw churned. Randy could feel the pulse of the engine once more. The boat was shaken with several sharp lurches. Then, as she became synchronized to her new motion, the engines began to throb with a strong, even beat.

"Mac did it again!" muttered the skipper.

"The old packet will need a complete overhaul when we

return."

"She'll get it," declared Castignoni.

The wind had risen to a fresh pitch, shrieking wrathfully. It sliced spindrift from the crested swells, driving it across the seas in smoking flurries. Wind-driven spray hammered the windows and streamed down the glass in sheets. Through the blurred panes Randy made out the swells, luminous with blue-green fire, climbing swiftly in great watery hills as if determined to crush the boat.

To shut out the sight, he spent more and more time watching the captain. Joe Castignoni stood with his stocky legs firmly planted on the duckboards, his hands white with their grip on the twisting wheel. When destructive stresses made the *Ripple's* stout timbers screech, the captain seemed to sense it with his hands, his arms and his legs. He would spin the wheel to ease the strain. A boat on automatic pilot at such a time, the boy realized, would have had her back broken because she'd be forcing her way through the seas rather than riding with them.

And though the captain might yet lose his battle and they might face the frying-pan-into-fire choice of remaining with a foundering vessel or attempting to launch small boats, Randy knew that such a defeat would be due to no fault of Joe Castignoni's. No skipper, he thought, could handle a boat with greater skill in such seas—not even Randy's own father.

Captain Castignoni had been so severe with the boy that Randy's feeling for the skipper had begun to change. But now, as he watched the master fighting hour after hour to save his ship, a begrudging admiration for the man came over him.

When dawn lighted the sullen gray skies, Randy knew the captain had won. The wind was not so fierce. Spray no longer beat the wheelhouse windows. And though the clipper still pitched and rolled in the enormous gray swells, the seas had lost their power of destruction.

At length the captain turned, his face gray and drawn with strain. "Did you learn anything?" he wearily asked Randy.

"Yes, sir. To make the seas work for you, not fight them!"

For a moment the expression of weariness left Joe Castignoni's face; he smiled faintly. "Take over, boy. Keep an eye on him, Steve."

Randy's mouth suddenly went dry. "In—in these seas, sir?"

"You don't become a rough-water helmsman taking the wheel on a calm day," snapped the skipper, stalking off to his room.

Randy's stomach tightened as he stepped onto the duckboards. Although the worst of the storm was past, he was afraid he might make some mistake that would bring the boat to disaster. When the vessel climbed a soaring swell, his knees would quake and he'd spin the wheel too far to port or to starboard, as he had when learning.

"Ease it off, Randy," Steve would say calmly. "Don't put too much pressure on the wheel. You don't want to break the shaft."

"I'll break something for sure!" Randy groaned.

"Joe wouldn't have let you take over if there'd been any

real danger of that. It's not as bad as it looks, but it's good experience."

Randy's steering soon improved under Steve's guidance, but he realized that he'd need a great deal of practice to make a good rough-water helmsman. Too frequently he'd fail to ease the strain on the wheel, and the clipper would shake from stem to stern, her propeller making the whole after-end tremble.

"You've had a long day," Steve said at last. "Like to go below and catch a little sleep?"

"I sure would, Steve!"

"Skip along, then. I don't think you'll need a rope now."

The *Ripple* still rolled in wide arcs when Randy stepped from the wheelhouse. He paused to look down upon the deck below. It was damp, but not much water flowed in the scuppers.

Awkward from fatigue and thinking of nothing but the opportunity to sleep, Randy hastily descended the stairs and started aft. There appeared to be no necessity to grip the grab-rail running along the bulkhead. Randy was too inexperienced to realize that even after the worst of a storm, an occasional large swell might be encountered.

The vessel suddenly plunged while starting a roll to port. Randy reached for the grab-rail, but before he could put his hand on it he was flung across the deck and struck the gunwale.

He was annoyed at his own carelessness, but he was not aware of any serious danger until a sea washed over the port side. The surge swept him from his feet, driving him against the bulkhead with a stunning impact. Then as the *Ripple* continued her port roll, the wash carried him in that direction.

He grasped at the gunwale, but the force of the water streaming over the side loosened his hold. The next moment he was in the ocean.

CHAPTER SEVEN

Boy Overboard!

RANDY GAVE an involuntary gasp as he plunged into the sea, and swallowed a mouthful of brine. A few quick strokes brought him to the surface, choking and coughing. He saw the stern of the *Ripple* gliding by.

"Man overboard!" he shouted in sudden panic. When his cry brought no one out on deck, he raised his voice in a piercing scream: "Help! Help! Steve—*help!*"

Everyone aboard was asleep except the engineer, his assistant and the navigator, and only the latter might have heard him. But the clashing of the seas, the creaking of the boat, the sound of the engines drowned out Randy's voice.

He uttered one final, despairing cry as the boat pulled away to the southward. And then, more from desperation than with any distinct purpose, he began to swim after the clipper. Though he knew he could not overtake her, he could think of nothing else to do.

A more immediate peril soon drove thoughts of the disappearing tuna boat from Randy's mind. A great sea was curling and about to break over him. Ton's of water would fall upon him with crushing force!

But as the sea started to cascade with a thunderous roar, Randy recalled Steve Vardon's story of the fisherman swept overboard from the *Westwind,* who had saved himself by diving when the swells broke. He drove himself down as the fisherman had done. Seconds later he felt a concussion on his body. Strong currents tumbled him over and over, though without doing him serious harm.

But when Randy came up for air and something struck his arm with an impact that momentarily dazed him, he was terrified. Dangerous sharks, he knew, inhabited these waters. Presently, brought up by a rising swell, he looked about anxiously but could see no sign of a fin. As he began to descend swiftly with the receding water, he drew several quick breaths. But he delayed his next dive until the sea started to break over him once more.

Upon returning to the surface again, Randy caught a fleeting glimpse of a dark, oblong object outlined against a smother of foam. It vanished into the trough before he could determine what it might be. He suspected it was the object that had struck his arm.

Randy gave up any idea of following the *Ripple*. He was having enough trouble merely to stay afloat. And now, during the moments when he was not diving to avoid breaking seas, he began to make plans.

Two hours would pass before his mates went to the galley for breakfast. Randy doubted if anyone would miss him until then. If the clipper turned about without delay and was able to retrace her course, four hours would elapse before he would be rescued. But Randy knew there was little hope that a vessel could return on a straight course in such seas. It seemed unlikely that he'd be found for at least eight hours.

That realization dashed the boy's spirits. He remembered

stories his father had told of different tuna fishermen who had been washed overboard. Some of those men had been lucky enough to remain afloat until they were picked up, and a few others had reached shore. Randy decided that the survivors must have conserved their strength. Now, to better face the ordeal ahead, Randy slipped off his heavy boots and peeled off all clothing except his shorts.

Swimming then required less effort. But it taxed his strength even to swim. He saw that when he was not diving to escape breaking seas, he must float. The less energy he spent, the greater would be his chance of surviving until the *Ripple* found him!

But something happened then to change Randy's mind. He saw the rectangular object once more, tilted against the sky. He watched for it to be overturned as it reached the crest of a swell. However, it slid from sight without changing position. Randy began to wonder how such a raft could stay together during a *chubasco*. It must be of stout construction, and its ability to remain upright in heavy seas made it a worthy craft.

It might keep him afloat until he could be rescued!

Randy struck out in the direction it had taken. Twice he was forced to dive to avoid breaking seas before he made out the raft once more, rising against the sky. He started a fast crawl to overtake it. When he was swept upward on a swell, however, he saw the raft climbing on another sea, as far away as ever.

Though he was tossed continuously by the swells, and often obliged to submerge to avoid injury, Randy continued the chase. Minutes would pass when he could not see the object of his blind pursuit. Then he would locate the raft again and strike out with fast strokes to reach it. The warning *crack* of a splintering sea would require another hurried dive each time he was within yards of the craft. And meanwhile the spurts and the punishment taken when the currents tumbled him over were rapidly draining away his strength.

Randy considered letting the raft go. But he had expended so much energy trying to overtake it that he dared not give up now. He was so close to exhaustion that he knew he would soon drown unless he could pull himself up onto the elusive platform of boards.

The knowledge that he must reach the raft or perish now spurred Randy to a final burst of exertion. He swam with strong, determined strokes, trying to keep the raft in sight. A big swell lifted him, and when it flowed with a rush beneath him he saw the wooden craft but a few yards away. Somehow he summoned the strength to give a few hard kicks. His hand closed on smooth boards.

Almost immediately a rushing swell snatched the raft. And then, while the boy's remaining energy ebbed away, the ocean seemed to be playing one last cruel jest. Each time Randy was nearly close enough to touch the raft, a sea would carry it away. His arms and legs felt too heavy to lift, but he doggedly forced himself to take one more stroke, then another and another. . . .

When he felt himself sinking from sheer exhaustion, Randy took what he believed would be his last spurt. To his surprise, he overtook the raft. He pressed his hands on the slippery boards, but with nothing he could take hold of, his palms would slide. Randy's dazed mind grasped the chilling truth. He was too tired to climb onto the craft after having reached it!

Slowly he slid back into the sea. Somewhere behind him he heard a swell cannonading, but he lacked the strength to dive. His hands continued to slip until they left the boards. He had barely started to sink when there came an unexpected reprieve.

The clashing and roaring Randy had heard was farther astern than he had realized. The sea broke well behind him, but he was caught in the foaming upsurge that followed. Powerful currents spun him in cartwheels, and when the roller washed over the raft, the boy was swept with it. Feeling something solid beneath his body, he spread-eagled his arms and legs to obtain as much purchase as possible.

And there he remained, gasping for breath, choking up the salt water he had swallowed. The seas sometimes gushed over him in streaming sheets. But more often the raft glided swiftly up the backs of the swells and then plunged into the troughs. For a while Randy feared the platform might turn turtle. But it did not. It rose and fell like a cork.

Slowly his strength returned, and he raised up on his elbows to examine the craft. It was painted black, the boards closely fitted. It was, in fact, a hatch cover! Perhaps it had been dislodged from one of the *Ripple's* holds to be carried overboard by the same sea that had lifted him over the rail. However that might be, it would not matter now if his mates took even a day or more to find him. His prospects were certainly not hopeless so long as he remained on the hatch cover!

In order to hold his position, Randy stretched out arms and legs to extend over as much of his make-shift raft as possible. As hour after hour passed, the seas moderated and it became less of a problem to stay aboard. After a while, he felt secure enough to sit up and glance around. The water had taken on a dull-gray tinge. When he looked up to discover the reason, he saw black clouds spreading across the sky.

Presently lightning forked through the sullen overcast, followed by a sharp clap of thunder. Minutes later there was a hard patter of rain. It was the prelude to a tropical cloudburst. When the skies opened the rain fell not in drops, not in sheets; it came bucketing down with the fierce beat of a waterfall. It flattened the seas. It obscured everything in a gray, driving pall. It pounded Randy until his body was numb and chilled.

The deluge did not last long. After the storm passed to the northwest, the heavens began to clear. The sun appeared and the sea steamed. The raft rolled gently in long, lazy swells. Randy felt that it was now safe to stand for a better view, but the rising mists still made it impossible to see far in any direction. He could not even make out the Mexican coast somewhere off to the southeast.

Throughout the remainder of the day Randy watched anxiously for the *Ripple*. He caught no glimpse of her before the sun set in a blaze of glowing reds and yellows. Night, as it does in equatorial latitudes, fell suddenly. The sea darkened until its inky depths seemed to hold countless drowned stars. The light southeasterly breeze was tempered by the land warmth for a while, but as the hours advanced the air grew uncomfortably cool.

Chilled both by the brisk breeze and by the washes splashing over the hatch cover, Randy grew so cold that his teeth chattered. He beat his arms around his bare body, and longed for the clothes he had discarded. Constantly his mind played with thoughts of a warm meal.

Schools of fish stirred flashes of phosphorescence as they passed the raft. Randy was so hungry that he began to snatch at these fish in the hope of obtaining food. They darted away when his hand plunged into the water, or wriggled loose when his fingers closed on one. As dawn was breaking, however, he scooped a tiny silver fish onto the raft. It flopped in a small flurry, and Randy struck it twice to avoid losing it. He had no way to cook it. But knowing that the Japanese sometimes ate raw fish, he munched it slowly to make the morsel of food last as long as possible.

The sun soon rose, thawing Randy's chilled body. Only a few wisps of cloud flecked the lightening sky. Across the glassy, rolling swells to the eastward, the low, brown ridge of the Mexican mountains was visible. And to the southeast, where Cape Corrientes marked the southern end of the Gulf of California, he made out a smudge of smoke that might be a steamship.

As the morning advanced, Randy stood up occasionally to scan the horizon. The dot of smoke had moved farther to the northward each time he looked. He realized it must be from a coasting vessel sailing into the gulf. Later he sighted the black funnels of another vessel, hull down to the westward.

His failure to see the *Ripple* worried the boy, and he wondered if his mates were still searching for him.

Before long sea gulls were circling his raft, mewling mournfully. Venturesome birds sometimes glided low, legs dangling as if about to alight, but the gulls always changed their minds, flying off again with a strong beat of wings. Randy hoped these circling birds might attract the attention of Jack Lucca if the *Ripple* were somewhere near at hand. Gulls were so commonly seen above schools of fish, however, that the mastman might attach no special importance to those hovering over the raft.

As the sun rose, like a molten copper disk in the cloudless sky, the searing heat became almost unbearable. The fierce rays scorched Randy's flesh; turn as he would, he could not escape them. The glare from the water burned him when the sun itself did not. Thirst became a torment as the sun mounted in the heavens, blazing white-hot upon his reddening skin, igniting the swells with a silvery fire.

At midday Randy heard a buzzing no louder than a distant swarm of bees. Not until the sound had grown louder, and was accompanied by an echoing clap on the water, did he realize what caused it. His blood quickened with excitement, and he stood up on the raft. In the blazing sky to the southward he saw a glittering silver speck.

Sure that it was the *Ripple's* scouting plane, the boy removed his shorts and began to wave in frantic wig-wags to attract Steve Vardon's attention. The plane held to its course; the clapping grew deafening as it approached. Then it flashed by, less than six miles to the eastward of the raft. A feeling of despair shot through Randy as he watched the plane continuing its flight northward.

In his bitter disappointment he blamed Steve for not keeping a sharper look-out. But he soon forgave his friend. At the altitude Steve was flying the raft would be no larger than a dot, and the white shorts no more conspicuous than a fleck of spindrift. Sunlight glinting from the water would also make it difficult to see.

The plane buzzed southward a quarter-hour later. Again Randy tried to catch Steve's eye, but the pilot failed to notice the white piece of fabric flagging on the water. As the boy replaced his shorts, he spied a gray fin near the raft.

Earlier that morning Randy had noticed sharks' fins slicing through the swells, but at such a great distance that he had felt no concern. This shark had seen him! Randy was chilled by a brief glimpse of the creature's sharp, vicious teeth as it raised its snout. Flicking its caudal fin, the shark jarred the raft as it passed underneath. Seconds later it reappeared on the opposite side. It swam in short, excited dashes that sent the water rippling away. Now and then it bumped the hatch cover and then streaked off, only to return moments afterward. Its peculiar gyrations attracted a second shark. Both predators grazed the raft or struck it with their tails as they dashed about in frenzied circles.

Randy was certain the big fish acted more from instinct than reason. Yet they seemed to know that prey might sometimes be obtained by bumping floating objects. Randy suspected that they were trying to upset the raft to hurl him into the water. Terrified lest they succeed, he sat in the center of the hatch cover, drawing up his knees to put as much space as possible between himself and the ugly creatures stalking him.

One by one, other sharks joined the pack, until six of the dread scavengers were swimming nearby. Numbers made them bolder. They butted the raft from one side, then the other. The impacts sometimes threw Randy off-balance. When he put out a hand to brace himself, one or more of the sharks would break water as though expecting him to fall overboard. Shaken with fright, the boy attempted to squeeze himself into a smaller space on the wooden platform.

In mid-afternoon the *Ripple's* monoplane flew northward again, but passed far to the west of Randy. With seven sharks now circling about him, the boy did not dare stand up and wave. With troubled eyes he watched Steve make a wide sweep to the north, and then fly southward over Mexican coastal waters.

A feeling of desolation took possession of Randy. Steve had not seen him. And perhaps this was the last search he would make. The seas had been too rough the previous day to launch a plane. And now the pilot must believe that looking for a swimmer was at best a forlorn hope. He'd have no way of knowing that Randy was on a raft.

The boy's chance of being found by a passing vessel was also dwindling. A steady southeast wind was making the raft drift farther and farther from the Mexican coast.

Late in the afternoon Randy had proof that his mates had not entirely abandoned hope of finding him. The monoplane made one more search flight that day. On one leg of its flight it buzzed directly over him. The boy risked an attack by the sharks when he stood up and waved. However, Steve failed to see the tiny dot on the sea.

The gulls flew away at sunset. And soon afterward the sharks tired of their futile attacks and vanished as well. Before the red glow faded from the western sky, Randy spent many uncomfortable minutes watching what appeared to be another predatory creature. When the raft drifted close to it, he discovered that it was only a long-handled brush, of the type used to swab decks. Since it might prove useful as a weapon, he salvaged it.

The cool breeze of evening was welcome after the boiling sub-tropical sun. But when a chill wind began blowing, Randy was forced to curl up into a ball to keep warm. The seas were soon breaking over the raft, and they felt like ice water on his sunburned flesh. Randy spent another wretched night flailing his cold body with his arms.

When the next blazing day began, the wind was still strong and the seas were frosted with spume. The big swells discouraged sharks, and only one hovered nearby. The beast was made wary by the erratic rising and falling of the hatch cover, however, and did not attempt to butt it.

A few sea gulls volplaned overhead, despite the strong wind, and Randy would hold his breath each time one showed signs of roosting on the raft. The birds always flapped aloft before they were within reach. The boy was so weak with hunger that even the tough flesh of a gull would have been welcome fare.

After many disappointments, he had so little hope of obtaining a meal in this way, that he scarcely noticed a big male bird that soared twice over the raft. He was startled to feel the sea gull settle on his head. It was still moving its pinions to balance itself when Randy's hands shot up swiftly to grasp the bird's legs. Wings beat his face. The gull's sharp beak slashed his forearms, but the boy refused to release his grip. He pushed the bird down onto the boards and quickly ended its struggles.

Ravenous with hunger, Randy tore away feathers and skin, while the gulls swooped about his head, uttering shrill, angry cries. As he finished cleaning the bird, he remembered that he must wait for the animal heat to leave its body before eating.

He cast over the refuse. Suddenly the water was lashed to foam by sharks darting back and forth past the raft. They twisted and turned to seize the insides, the skin and feathers of the gull. And then, their appetites still unsatisfied, they began to jar the craft with hard flicks of their caudal fins. Thoroughly alarmed, Randy picked up the long-handled brush he had fished from the sea and brought it down on the nose of a shark. It sent the water swirling in a sudden dive. One by one, the boy dealt each of the big scavengers the same treatment, until they kept their distance.

After a while, Randy ripped away a piece of the gull's flesh with his teeth. It was tough and had a fishy taste. He had to chew slowly because of his thirst-swollen tongue. The juices he extracted from the meat, however, made his mouth and throat feel less parched. Hungry though he was, Randy could eat only a little of the stringy, unpalatable flesh. But he kept the remainder to nibble at whenever he could find the appetite for it.

All day Randy watched for the monoplane, though he knew there was little chance that it could take off while the seas were so heavy. His failure to see the plane nevertheless made his spirits sink. He was sure that he had been given up for lost.

As dusk gathered over the ocean once more, he felt completely abandoned. The seething and swishing of the seas had partially deafened him, so that he failed to hear a distant *chug-chug-chug*. The sound eventually captured his attention, however, and he sat up with a start. A shiver darted down his spine. What he heard was the throbbing of an engine. A vessel was approaching!

Randy braced his legs to stand, trying to see beyond the tossing swells. He could not even make out a light, but the sound of a pulsing engine grew louder. He removed his shorts in order to signal.

And then, through the purpling haze Randy made out a slender figure in a crow's nest. The figure appeared and vanished with the swaying of the mast, but the vessel beneath was not visible.

"Jack!" the boy shouted hoarsely, waving the white garment. "Jack Lucca! *Jack Lucca!*"

The clashing of the seas smothered his voice. It was clear that the mastman failed to hear his cry, for he turned to peer off to the westward. Desperately Randy shouted and waved.

But Lucca did not face about. His slim figure grew dim against the fading afterglow in the western sky. Then it could no longer be seen, and the sound of the *Ripple's* engines dwindled and died away.

CHAPTER EIGHT

Rugged Fishing on

the Iron Rack

WHAT IMPULSE caused Jack Lucca to turn and sweep the seas to the southeastward a second time, Randy would never know. But he did look back, and his glass picked out the moving fleck of white on the darkened sea.

Lucca kept his binoculars trained on the spot. But when he saw nothing more, he imagined that the flash of white had been a trick of his strained and blood-shot eyes. He had been in the crow's nest from dawn to dark since the moment it was discovered that Randy was missing.

Later the mastman would admit that he had hesitated to ask Captain Castignoni to turn back. A hundred times since the boat had zigged northward in search of Randy, Lucca had reported flashes that had proved to be spindrift or flotsam.

The mastman knew that the search would end with the coming of complete darkness that evening. For that reason he was unwilling to pass up what might be his last chance to find Randy. He requested the skipper to retrace his course. . . .

Randy had dropped to the raft with a feeling of utter despair after the clipper vanished. Believing that he had now lost all chance of rescue, he was astonished minutes later to see the swaying mast reappear. His heart gave a bound. For the boat was heading directly toward him!

Excitedly he waved the pair of shorts. Above the throbbing of the engine and the clashing of the waves Jack Lucca's shout reached him: "Someone's waving, Captain! It must be Randy!"

The boy's throat was tight as he slipped on his shorts and waited. Presently the *Ripple* glided along the windward side of the raft, churning suds astern. All the fishermen leaning over the rail, with two exceptions, were laughing and yelling. However, the Captain's son was turning the Navajo bracelet on his wrist, a frown on his saturnine face. And tears streamed down little Julio Ortorio's weathered brown cheeks, while his long, white mustache quivered with emotion.

"My young friend—!" Ortorio began, then his voice broke.

Someone cast a rope, and Randy made it fast around the hatch cover before reaching for the willing hands waiting to help him aboard. Steve Vardon noticed the boy's blistered skin and warned the men back when they appeared about to embrace him.

"Take it easy, boys!" he shouted. "Randy's cooked to a crisp!"

Joe Castignoni, having put the vessel on automatic pilot, now hurried aft. Emotion was visible in his strong, brown face.

"Didn't know how I'd ever break it to your parents if we failed to find you." His gruff tone could not conceal his feeling. "Come up to my room. We've got to do something about that bad sunburn."

Castignoni glanced at the cook, and George Terraza seemed to understand what was needed, for he said, "I'll bring up a glass of water and some warm soup to your quarters, Joe."

The captain nodded and started forward. Upon reaching his room, he mixed several liquids in an atomizer bottle, shook it thoroughly, and sprayed the medication over Randy's skin. It must have contained menthol, for it caused a freezing sensation, but within a few minutes the boy began to feel more comfortable.

As the treatment ended, Steve Vardon appeared with the cook. Terraza had brought a glass of water and a cup of soup. Randy gulped down both, and wished there were more.

"Even sheets will feel hot on that skin, Randy," Steve observed.

"I'll be all right now, Steve," the boy said.

"If your blistered skin doesn't become infected," murmured the captain, frowning. He glanced thoughtfully at Randy for several moments, and then turned to the navigator. "He's got to stay out of the sun and lie quiet, Steve, but he'd find his bunk too hot. I picked up a soft, open-work Mexican hammock at Manzanillo several years back, and it's still stowed in the net locker. See if you can't find some way to rig it up under the after-deck overhang. Randy would be in the shade there."

"I'll take care of it," said Steve.

When he and the cook left the bridge, the captain turned

to Randy. "We'd have abandoned the search long before we did if it hadn't been for the missing hatch cover. I thought it might have washed overboard when you did."

"I guess it did," said Randy. "I sure thought that I'd never be found when Steve flew close several times and couldn't see me."

"A raft is a mighty small object to spot from the air." The skipper smiled wryly. "No one knows that better than I do! Once eight men and I clung to the partly submerged hull of a tuna boat for thirty-six hours. Coast Guard search planes passed overhead but mistook the bottom of our boat for a rock. Three of my mates were lost before a tuna clipper found us."

Randy suspected that he owed his life to the captain's experience. For Joe Castignoni, still haunted by the memory of those terrible hours in the sea, had continued looking for Randy long after another master would have given up.

Randy thanked the skipper for his treatment, and went aft to find Steve and several other men tightening the ropes of a hammock. It was suspended from big hooks screwed into the out-jutting floor of the main deck, this overhang shielding it from the sun. It was the large type of hammock used in the warmer regions of Mexico in lieu of a bed—of an open weave and rich yellow in color, with slightly curving braces at either end to prevent it from folding in upon its occupant.

"Hop in, Randy," said Steve. "Let's see how you look."

"Tie him in," growled Louie, "so he won't fall overboard again."

Ignoring the taunt, Randy sat in the middle of the hammock and swung his legs into the center. He winced when his sunburned flesh pressed the soft, open strands. Yet he knew that the skipper could have thought of no way to make him more comfortable. Air circulated freely about his body, and he did not have to brace against the rolling of the boat because gravity held him in an almost stationary position.

"It's super, Steve!" the boy said gratefully.

He fell into a drugged slumber the moment the men left him, for he had had little sleep on the raft. George Terraza awakened him several hours later when he brought a nourishing oyster stew. That was the last thing Randy remembered until the following morning, when he opened his eyes and found that one of his mates had covered him with a sheet.

His body burned like fire when he got up to join the others for breakfast. After the meal and another treatment he returned to the hammock.

The next days were miserable ones for Randy. Any position he chose brought some portion of his blistered body in painful contact with the hammock. He felt feverish. Large patches of skin began to peel, and the flesh beneath was red and sometimes festered. Fearful of infection, the skipper continued his program of medication.

But for an active boy like Randy, the enforced idleness was harder to bear than the sunburn. Captain Castignoni would not allow him to resume his duties because that would expose his skin to sunlight. Randy could not even fly with Steve. And only after a new and healthy skin replaced the old one was he permitted to take the wheel, during the midday hours, when the sun was overhead.

Throughout the period of Randy's convalescence the *Ripple* sailed southward along the coasts of El Salvador and Nicaragua. It was desolate country, and in only a few places had men fought back the jungle to build small towns, marked by iron piers thrust out into the open Pacific. Great combers beat high upon the gray sand beaches, and beyond lay the thick snarl of mangrove swamps, at the feet of towering green mountains. Rising above the lush slopes was an occasional white peak or the darker cones of still-active volcanoes. From the latter, white clouds of steam or billows of smoke mounted against the deep blue of the sky.

In this wild and sparsely settled country, Randy thought, the secret of the missing clipper *Westwind* might be found. Each time the scouting plane returned, the boy questioned Steve. But the pilot saw no signs of recent wreckage, though on two occasions he sighted the rotting hulks of tuna boats driven ashore by heavy ground swells in past years.

"You'd better not count on seeing Frank Castignoni again," Steve said gently the last time Randy inquired about wreckage.

The boy made no reply, but his jaw stiffened. He knew there was small chance he would still be alive if his mates had not continued their search long after little hope of finding him remained.

Fishing was poor, for the seas were so heavy that Steve Vardon could not often take off in the plane to scout for schools of tuna. The two schools he did find proved disappointing. One consisted of large yellowfins which refused both chums and lures. The other was a school of smaller two-pole tuna which mysteriously drifted away after the men had hauled in five tons of fish.

One day Captain Castignoni decided that Randy's skin could once more stand tropical sunlight. The boy was sent aloft to help Lucca find fish.

Quartering seas were making the *Ripple* roll and pitch when Randy scrambled up the rigging. The mastman caught his arm to steady him as he clambered into the small metal barrel.

"Take the glass," Lucca said. "I'm half-blinded."

Randy braced himself and raised the binoculars. There was not a cloud in the sky, and in the crystal-clear air the sunlight had a searing intensity. It played with dazzling brilliance across the mirrorlike swells, making them flash and glimmer. It glinted from the foaming, cascading crests of the sea until they glared with the white fire of a sunlit snowfield. The rolling of the vessel made all these points of brightness streak across Randy's vision. When he lowered his lids, his light-satiated eyes still seemed to be seeing scores of scintillating flashes. Before long he imagined that he could make out schools of tuna, roiling the water, blazing in the fierce sunlight, whichever way he looked.

He passed the glass back to Lucca, saying, "I prefer dark goggles."

"The wind cleared away every mist," Lucca explained. "But it's a warm wind, and even if it's stirring up a strong sea, we might find tuna."

Randy was doubtful about that, for he saw no sign of the porpoises, gulls or cormorants that usually indicated the presence of tuna.

While the mastman lowered his lids to rest his eyes, Randy observed a distant patch of foam glistening with rippling silvery lights. Even after a swell rolled over the spot, the water remained broken, flashing and foaming as before. He took the glass from Lucca and brought it to bear on the disturbed area. For hundreds of yards the ruffled sea flashed like diamonds, but the glare was so great that he could distinguish nothing clearly.

"If there were birds or porpoises over there," Randy said, pointing, "I'd say we'd spotted a school of tuna."

"You wouldn't find either when the wind is this strong and the seas so heavy." The mastman took the glass and studied the water. Suddenly he raised his voice in a shout: "Tuna—six points to port!"

"How do you know, Jack?" Randy asked in a puzzled tone.

"In time you recognize the signs, Randy."

Down below men were pounding forward to confirm the mastman's announcement. The captain and Steve Vardon stepped from the wheelhouse, the latter taking charge of the small remote-control steering device.

"Half a point more to port," Lucca called out.

Castignoni glanced up. "Big ones, Lucca?"

Lucca lowered the glass, a shy, self-conscious smile flitting across his face. "Skipjacks, I'm afraid."

A chorus of groans came from below. The smaller striped tuna known as skipjacks brought less than the light-meat yellowfins. They were more likely to spoil on a long voyage.

Canneries of late had objected to buying skipjacks, even at their lower price.

"All mastmen are crazy," said Freshwater good naturedly. "Jack sees some small yellowfins."

But the men watched anxiously as the vessel chugged toward the ruffled patch of sea. Presently Randy saw fish darting across their course. And soon he spied the silver or purple blazes of fish breaking water. They appeared to be medium-sized tuna, probably twenty-pounders, and he suspected that they were not yellowfins.

Suddenly Nicco Puccinelli wailed. "Skips!" he cried in disgust.

The elation usually visible in the men's faces upon finding tuna was missing now. They looked questioningly at the captain.

"Will the cannery take them if we bring them in?" Steve asked.

"I agreed not to take any skips unless fishing was poor," Joe Castignoni said after a long pause. "Well, it couldn't be much worse! If we don't take over a tenth of our catch in skipjacks, the cannery probably won't fuss too much."

Randy foresaw trouble when he and the others swung the iron fishing racks over the side. Each roll of the boat plunged the grilled bottom from sight, and allowed the seas to break over the racks. But none of the fishermen seemed to consider it too rough for fishing.

Steve Vardon saw the boy's doubtful expression and laughed. "Afraid you'll get your feet wet?"

"Not only my feet!" Randy said with a rueful grin.

Doc Bernedetto put a crowder in one tank to compress the chums into smaller space, and began to strew bait upon the seas. Skipjacks broke water to seize the bait.

Hurriedly the men found their single-pole rigs and dropped over the portside. Even with one knee braced against the low rail of the rack, Randy found it hard to keep his balance. The starboard rolling of the vessel hurled him back against the hull. And when the *Ripple* heeled to port, he was flung forward and plunged waist-deep into the water.

"Randy's scared of a little spray," Louie shouted acidly. "Anyone got a dry towel for him?"

Randy's cheeks burned at the men's laughter. He cast his feathered lure into the milling, flashing school of fish. Skipjacks at first ignored his squid as well as those of his mates. Then Tony Riggio's pole bent suddenly with a strike. Fishermen yelled as he sent the tuna arching over the rail to thump the bait tank.

Louie whooped as he whipped a striped tuna over his head. Randy's pole bobbed, and he lashed back to skim his fish over the rail. Presently there was a constant *thump-thump-thump* of skipjacks hitting the tank.

As a rule fishermen regarded one-pole tuna fishing as sport because they were not obliged to time their strikes to those of one or more partners. Hook-and-line fishing in heavy seas, however, was always drudgery.

To Randy, who was unfamiliar with such conditions, it was a nightmare. Sometimes he was plunged to his armpits in the sea while trying to boat a fish. And when gray fins began to cleave the water, he found it hard to overcome a feeling of panic. The rail of the rack dipped below the surface on each port roll, and then there was nothing to prevent a shark from reaching him. His mates appeared to be well aware of this danger. Occasionally a fisherman would slip a pole from the socket of his leather waist pad and drive the end against the snout of a shark venturing too close. But the men seemed to look upon the big scavengers as a normal risk. Randy, after his experience on the raft, could not do so. He loathed the ugly creatures.

Perhaps an hour passed before the clipper lost contact with the school. While the captain was locating it again, the men stowed away their catch, which had mounted between the bait tank and the rail. Every skipjack had been dumped into a fish well by the time the skipper had the boat set once more on automatic pilot and came aft.

Randy and the others resumed their work. Fish slime dripping from the stern of the vessel had attracted more sharks. The boy had to strike one of the vicious fish from time to time to discourage its close approach.

He had become adjusted to the weight of the tuna in this particular school. He knew what force to apply to use the drive of a skipjack's strike to assist him in swinging it aboard. Only rarely was there a difference of even a few pounds between the largest and smallest fish in a school. But there were exceptions to this rule; stray fish would at times join another group. If the intruding fish was a large yellowfin, fishermen, unprepared for its violent strike, were caught unawares.

That now happened to Randy.

· 152 ·

He had a fleeting glimpse of a large fish passing under the rack. He made the mistake of assuming that it was a shark, whereas it was in reality a four-pole tuna, separated from its own school. The yellowfin struck the lure while moving swiftly away from the rack rather than toward it. The pull was so sudden, so forceful, that the boy was catapulted over the rail.

As he plunged into the sea, Randy released his pole before the big fish could draw him away from the boat. Terrified by the thought that a shark might attack him before he could climb aboard, the boy lashed the water with desperate strokes. Swimming was made difficult by his rubber boots, which had filled with water.

The *Ripple* was recovering from a starboard roll when Randy broke water. He splashed wildly, unable to understand what had become of the rack. Too late he realized that it had been lifted clear of the water by the starboard heeling of the vessel. He had come up beneath it!

Before he could escape, the grilled bottom struck Randy's crash helmet. Lights burst before his eyes, and he was dimly aware of sinking. He was not, however, quite unconscious. Some instinct of preservation sounded a warning in his fogged mind. He sensed that he must slip out from under the fishing rack—or drown!

CHAPTER NINE

Medico Call for Louie

WHEN THE iron fishing rack descended on Randy's head, it drove his crash helmet over his ears and nose, making it impossible to see. His rubber boots, filled with water, were pulling him down. Dazed though he was, the boy sensed that he must rid himself of both encumbrances.

Bringing up first one knee and then the other, he tugged off the boots. Then he kicked to drive himself upward as he wrenched at his helmet. The moment it was gone, his head began to clear.

He saw the surface, rippling in silvery waves above him— the hull of the boat—the grilled fishing rack—and the skipjacks, flashing as they fought for chums.

And he saw something else that sent a chill through him. A black-tipped fin was moving between the skipjacks, and presently Randy spied the shark itself.

The hull of the rolling boat struck the boy. Instantly he flexed his legs and placed his feet against it. With this purchase, he pushed hard to force himself out from under the rack. At the same time, his hands lashed the water. He knew that no human swimmer could outdistance a shark in its own element. His only hope lay in climbing aboard before it saw him.

He popped up as a sea was breaking over the portside of

the vessel. Every man on the racks had put aside his pole and was extending a hand to assist him aboard. The boat recovered from her port roll as Randy reached for the nearest hand—and missed!

My last chance! he thought in panic.

But he failed to reckon on one circumstance. Usually his black hair was kept close-cropped, but it had grown somewhat long during his weeks at sea. This unavoidable neglect now proved his salvation. For the captain, at the risk of falling overboard, flung himself down on the low rail of the rack, and by a long reach managed to grasp the boy's thick locks. Randy thought his hair was being torn from his head when the captain abruptly straightened up.

Lifted by his scalp, Randy was swung to safety. And as his feet passed over the railing, he heard a sharp click behind him.

"Good work, Joe!" Riggio cried in a strained voice. "That shark's teeth missed Randy's feet by less than eight inches!"

"I'm stopping for coffee!" declared Steve huskily.

"We could all use a cup," said the captain. "That was too close!"

Randy's teeth chattered so badly that he was unable to thank the skipper. Castignoni gave him a slight push.

"Over the side, boy. We all get pulled off now and then. Forget it!"

Fishermen clambered over the vessel's rail and trudged wearily to the galley. They filled mugs from the big coffeepot on the stove, and the first men took places at the table, the late arrivals sipping the black brew standing.

Louie raised his big cup, and then lowered it so suddenly that coffee slopped over onto the table. Randy noticed the gray, drawn expression of Louie's face as he stared blankly at the spreading pool.

George Terraza mopped up the coffee. "What's wrong with you?" he asked crossly.

"I don't feel so good," muttered the captain's son.

"Give your place to someone else, then," snapped the cook.

The hulking youth groaned as he rose. He walked slowly from the galley without a word to anyone.

"Louie's not like you, Joe," observed Tony Riggio.

The captain shrugged. "He takes after his mother's side. My father-in-law, Primo Mazzanini, sometimes sulked for days."

"That tough old rooster!" said Riggio. "He ruled his five girls and seven boys with an iron hand. It's a wonder Mazzanini didn't try to run your home, too, Joe, after you married one of his daughters."

"He tried," said the captain dryly. "He didn't get far."

Randy recalled that Frank Castignoni had never been overly fond of his grandfather. Old Primo Mazzanini had been too stern, too severe, too unbending. He had made every decision for his family. Could that explain why Mrs. Castignoni was unable to meet the problems that arose in her home?

Still pondering that question, Randy washed his mug and went to his room for a spare crash-helmet.

He found Louie lying with knees drawn up, staring at the

· 156 ·

upper bunk above him. Beads of moisture had gathered on his strained face; his heavy lips were compressed and white.

"What's the matter?" Randy asked.

"Stomach-ache," Louie snapped.

"Can I get you anything?"

"Yes, you can get out and leave me alone."

Ignoring the other's rudeness, Randy stood staring down at Louie. Unable to think of any way to be helpful, he went to his locker for his crash-helmet. When he stepped outside, he almost collided with the skipper.

"I think Louie is sick, Captain."

The skipper went into the room, giving his son a long, searching glance. "What's the trouble, Louie?"

"I—I guess I had something for breakfast that didn't set right."

"Where does it hurt?"

Louie touched his right side. The captain pressed the spot. The sick youth moaned, and pushed his father's hand aside.

"Don't!" he groaned.

There was a frown on the captain's face when he glanced up.

"Good thing you called me, Randy. This isn't a stomach-ache. It's appendicitis." He turned to his son. "How long has it troubled you?"

"Off and on for months," said Louie thickly.

"Why didn't you tell me?"

"I thought it was something I'd eaten."

The captain started toward the door, saying, "Come along, Randy. You'd better learn how to send a Medico."

The term was familiar to the boy. A "Medico" was a radio appeal for medical assistance from vessels which carried no ship's doctor to others which did. Doctors answering the call would describe what treatment a sick or injured man should receive. In extreme cases they would even direct a captain or a mate by radio through every step of an emergency operation.

When the captain reached his room, he began to tap out the code signal for a Medico. He was obliged to repeat the call a number of times before there was an answering *dash-dot-dash,* which meant, "Go ahead." Randy's knowledge of International Morse was so meager that he could not follow the swift exchange of code between Captain Castignoni and another vessel's radio operator.

But at last the skipper looked up. "I'm talking with the *S.S. Valparaiso.*" He sighed with relief, and added, "She carries a surgeon."

The other operator now switched to voice transmission and carried on an informal conversation with Joe Castignoni while they waited for the *Valparaiso's* doctor to reach the radio shack.

"This is Doctor Tomlinson, Captain," a voice presently announced. "Will you please describe your son's condition?"

Castignoni did so.

The ship's doctor asked the *Ripple's* position. Then, after questioning the radio operator about medical facilities at different ports, he suggested that Louie be kept in ice packs until the clipper could reach Puntarenas.

"But from what you tell me, Captain," Dr. Tomlinson concluded, "you might not reach port in time. I'd better describe the steps of an appendix operation—in case we lose contact with you."

Randy pushed a pad before Joe Castignoni. The skipper picked up a pencil and said hoarsely, "Go ahead, Doctor."

Randy's mind was in such a confused whirl that he heard little of what was being said. He was stunned by the idea of Captain Castignoni, with no medical training whatsoever, undertaking surgery on his own son.

After signing off, the skipper asked, "Did you follow that?"

"My—my mind must have been wandering, sir."

A frown creased the captain's brow. "You would have done well to pay attention," he said curtly. "You might face this yourself some day."

What did he mean, Randy wondered. Only the captain or the navigator performed the medical duties on a tuna boat.

"Did the doctor think Louie's appendix might burst?" the boy asked anxiously.

"Not if we can reach a doctor in time. And I certainly hope we can! Surgery is not in my line." He strode out to the bridge wing and shouted, "Fishing's over, boys. Hoist the racks and stow away the skipjacks. We're making a fast run to Puntarenas."

Having followed the captain outside, Randy now headed for the ladder.

"Not you," said Castignoni. "You have another job."

Leading the way into his room, he pulled out one of the

medical-supply drawers and removed a red rubber bag. It resembled a hot-water bottle, except for the large screw top in the center.

"Fill this with ice, and place it on the right side of Louie's abdomen. Replace the ice as it melts. Keeping his appendix chilled, the doctor said, might prevent it from rupturing."

Steve stood in the doorway, his cap pushed back. Sensing an emergency, he turned without a word and walked briskly to the wheel.

The clipper pounded along at full speed by the time Randy reached the galley. He carried a tray of ice cubes to the sink, loosened the chunks and pushed the pieces through the bag's opening.

Upon entering his room, he saw that Louie's eyes were closed and his face contorted from suffering. He unbuckled Louie's belt, pulled up his shirt and slid the bag gently into place.

"Can't you leave me alone?" Louie demanded fretfully.

"Louie, if this icebag prevents your appendix from bursting, your father won't have to operate."

The big youth opened tortured eyes. "That bad?" he asked dully.

Randy unbuttoned Louie's shirt to allow the soft breeze to play over his perspiring chest. The grayness of his patient's face worried him. There was nothing he could do, however, except replace ice in the bag at regular intervals.

At length the captain appeared. His face was troubled as he felt Louie's hot forehead and shifted the icebag slightly.

"How are you feeling, Son?" he asked.

"It doesn't hurt—quite so much, Papa."

"I hope we can reach a doctor within three hours. We're getting everything we can out of the Diesels."

"Three hours!' Louie groaned, and closed his eyes.

Randy thought the waiting would never end.

But at last he saw through the open doorway the prominent white cape, marked "Cabo Blanco" on the chart, and stepped outside. The *Ripple* sped past Isla Blanca, on its western side, then glided through the broad entrance of the Gulf of Nicoya. Rising above the beautiful landlocked bay to the eastward were the Herradura Mountains. And in the distance, surmounting them, were higher volcanic peaks.

The clipper soon threaded her way between the small, wooded isles dotting the bay. Although Randy would have liked to linger on deck to see more, he reluctantly returned to his room to bathe Louie's face and refill the icebag.

Before long there was a shrill *wheet-wheet-wheet* of a whistle, and the *Ripple* drifted to a stop. Randy looked out and saw a government launch skimming alongside. A minute later four uniformed Costa Ricans came aboard. Captain Castignoni shook their hands and then tersely described his son's condition. The health officer came to look at Louie and confirm the skipper's statement that his son's illness was not of a contagious nature. He and two of the other officers then quickly finished their business and returned to the launch. The fourth Costa Rican, a pilot, was left aboard to take the clipper to her mooring.

When Randy stepped outside again the *Ripple* was sailing past a long, L-shaped mole or breakwater, extending from the eastern end of a narrow peninsula. Puntarenas sprawled westward along this peninsula, an unattractive collection of musty shacks and buildings separated by sandy streets. The clipper rounded the point of the breakwater and chugged slowly by two cargo ships lying at anchor. Both vessels were taking aboard green stems of bananas from lighters. On the larger of the two wharves sheltered by the breakwater, were box-cars from which brown-skinned natives were removing emerald fruit to load other lighters. Apparently the two "banana boats" were of too deep draft to run alongside either wharf, but the *Ripple,* drawing less water, was taken up to the larger pier by her Cost Rican pilot.

Within the past few minutes the sun had vanished and a sullen overcast now shrouded the sky. The humid air was scented with brine and oil and the decaying odor of the not far distant jungle. Large drops of rain began falling as Ortorio and Puccinelli scrambled up the wharf ladder to secure the mooring lines. Seconds later a tropical downpour beat like wooden mallets upon the deck.

Despite the hard rain, the captain and the native pilot splashed past Randy's room, ascended to the wharf and hurried toward the town.

Castignoni reappeared minutes later with another Costa Rican who carried a small, black bag. The men came immediately to the room where Randy was caring for his patient. The visitor was short and stocky, and there was a kindly warmth in his olive-skinned face and large brown eyes.

"This is Dr. Alvarez, Randy," explained the skipper.

The doctor's white teeth flashed beneath a neat gray mustache; he bowed slightly before turning to remove the ice-bag from Louie's abdomen. Though he probed gently, a low, moaning sound escaped the sick youth's tight lips. Dr. Alvarez quickly concluded his examination and replaced the icebag.

"His appendix hasn't burst yet, Doctor?" the captain inquired with anxiety.

"No, no, *Capitán!*" And the doctor hesitated. "But in my mind is this question: do we dare risk a delay in operating?"

"*Delay!*" echoed Castignoni. "Is no bed to be had in the San Rafael Hospital here? Won't they take seamen?"

"They will, *Capitán,* and there are beds." Dr. Alvarez pushed out his lips, frowning. "But if there is time, it would be wiser to send your son to the capital, to San José. Either the Hospital of San Juan de Deos or the Chaqui Hospital is better equipped for surgical work. Myself, I would recommend Dr. Perez of the Chaqui Hospital."

"But it's seventy-three miles to San José!" protested Castignoni.

Dr. Alvarez thrust out his lips and drew a large, old-fashioned gold watch from his pocket. "A train leaves in twenty-seven minutes. If your son is kept packed in icebags, I believe it will be safe."

The captain's face was troubled. "I don't see how I can accompany my son. I'm responsible for my boat and crew. Nor can I spare my navigator. Freshwater? Ortorio? Riggio? They speak no Spanish. . . ."

He broke off abruptly, staring at Randy.

"You'll take Louie to San José!"

A chill wind blew through the boy. He stared aghast at the skipper. The man's grave face told him that he must be responsible for the big, surly youth on the trip to San José. The possibility that Louie's appendix might burst on the way to the capital frightened Randy.

"Come along," said the captain gruffly, as if the matter were already settled. "You'll need money for expenses."

Freshwater, Julio Ortorio, Tony Riggio and George Terraza stood outside in the driving downpour.

"How is Louie?" Freshwater asked with concern.

"He's going to San José for an operation," declared the captain. "Pack bags for him and for Randy, Freshwater. . . . Terraza, fill a bucket with ice cubes."

As the two fishermen hurried to do his bidding, Randy followed the skipper to his room. Castignoni twirled the dials of a small safe set in the bulkhead, swung back the door and lifted out a tin box. From it he removed a packet of bills. He counted out a number, and slipped the currency into an envelope.

"Don't lose this," he said, handing it to the boy. "You'll be paying all expenses. See that Louie has a good room and every service the doctor recommends. And find yourself a place to stay in some hotel near the Chaqui Hospital. This is placing a heavy load on your shoulders, Randy, but I think you can do the job."

The boy was turning to leave when the captain added, "There's good phone service from the capital to Puntarenas, I understand. Call me at the Customs House at seven tonight and let me know how things come out."

"Yes, sir. I will."

The rain had ceased as suddenly as it began. When Randy and the captain stepped outside, sunlight was slanting down through the parting clouds, making the wharf and the box-cars steam.

Dr. Alvarez had not been idle. By use of gestures and the few English words he knew, he was having six of the *Ripple's* crew raise Louie to the wharf in the same yellow hammock Randy had lain in while recovering from his severe sunburn. After this was done, the doctor brought his car out on the wharf and the patient was lifted into the back seat. The two sea bags and the bucket of ice also went into the sedan.

"Better come along, Freshwater," said the captain. "I'll need a hand with the hammock."

Dr. Alvarez drove slowly to spare his patient discomfort, and the car drew up to the station with only a minute to spare.

The captain handed a bill to the doctor. "Would you please get the tickets, Doctor?—Randy, grab those bags and the ice—Louie, climb out carefully and lower yourself onto the hammock— That's good, Son!—Hoist your end, Freshwater. We've got to burn our boilers to make it!"

The two stretcher-bearers almost ran with the hammock. Randy, burdened with two sea bags and the bucket of ice, tried to keep pace. To his surprise, there was a modern electric train on the tracks. The doctor dashed up with two tickets, which he handed to the boy.

Randy climbed aboard and hurried to the first two empty seats. He piled bags between them to serve as a make-shift bed. The captain and Freshwater lifted Louie onto it. Outside a trainman was shouting.

"This packet is about to slip her mooring lines," yelled Castignoni, seizing Freshwater's arm. "Good luck, Louie."

The two men bustled off the train only seconds before it began moving.

The rain-darkened wooden houses of Puntarenas quickly slipped past. Then the cars were clicking along between graceful coconut palms, their drooping fronds motionless in the dead, humid air.

A stubby conductor with a graying mustache appeared at the end of the car. *"Sirvanse monstrar los billetes, señores,"* he called out. And taking the first passenger's ticket, he punched it.

When he reached Randy's seat, the boy explained in halting Spanish that Louie required the extra seats because he was being taken to the hospital. "But I'll pay for them, *señor,"* he added.

"Nada! nada!" cried the conductor, with an expansive gesture to indicate the half-filled car. He punched the ticket, and then spoke so rapidly that Randy could not follow the words. He gathered, however, that the conductor wished to do anything he could to make Louie comfortable.

"You are very kind, *señor."*

"It is nothing, *mi amigo.* I myself have three sons."

The train now clicked along through banana *fincas,* these small ranches being divided by deep drainage ditches. Here and there Randy spied the white or yellow houses of the owners, shaded beneath great ceiba trees. Over the tracks,

· 166 ·

like a green canopy, stretched the large, flimsy leaves of towering banana plants.

Randy had little time to observe the passing country, however, for Louie was not standing the trip well. In the oppressive heat his clothing clung to his body, so that he twisted and squirmed with misery. The icebag did little to relieve his discomfort. No sooner was the rubber bag slipped between his shirt and his feverish body than the ice would start melting. Randy was kept busy running to the washroom to empty out the lukewarm water. He was alarmed at how fast the cubes were melting in the bucket.

Presently an elderly man of aristocratic appearance hobbled up with the aid of a cane, and paused to turn sympathetic eyes on Louie. With a slight bow, he said to Randy, "If there is anything I might do, *mi amigo,* it would be my pleasure to assist your friend."

A little flustered by the unexpected courtesy, Randy thanked the man and said he would call upon him should he need assistance. To his surprise, the other passengers came, one by one, to make the same offer.

Randy was grateful for the kindness and courtesy of these Costa Ricans, for they made him feel less like a stranger in an alien land.

Nevertheless, he was worried by the slow progress of the train, which was now climbing a steep mountain grade. That the tracks were an engineering feat, the boy was forced to acknowledge, for they were hewn from precipitous slopes, penetrated the dense tropical jungle and spanned white-water cataracts bounding in swift, rushing torrents to the sea.

Land-owners had reclaimed level portions of the mountains for coffee plantations, and the bushes stood in long, neat rows, their delicate foliage shielded from direct sunlight by banana plants or palms.

After a hard climb, the train reached a plateau, over-shadowed by the green slopes of high, volcanic peaks. The tempo of the car wheels quickened. Not many minutes later Randy saw cane huts and small stucco shacks flashing past the windows.

The conductor opened the car door and hurried up to speak to Randy. "This is San José," he explained. "Your friend will need help, *verdad?*"

Passengers who had previously found no way to assist the young Americans now crowded around Randy. He feared that so many willing but inexpert helpers might do Louie more harm than good.

As the train stopped, he caught sight of two white-uniformed men hurrying along the platform with a stretcher.

"*Momentito!*" he begged, and pushed through the crowd to hail the men from the steps of the car.

Reluctantly they approached. "We are sorry," one of them explained. "But we must find a *Señor* Draper."

"I'm Randy Draper!" the boy exclaimed in Spanish.

The faces of the men brightened, and the same man spoke once more: "Dr. Alvarez called from Puntarenas. He asked us to meet you."

When the two ambulance men boarded the car with their stretcher, passengers beamed with satisfaction to see the problem so neatly solved. Gentle though the two men were,

Louie clenched his teeth to prevent an outcry as they lifted him to the stretcher and carried him from the train to a waiting ambulance.

Randy climbed in back with the patient, and began a ride he would never forget. With siren wailing, the ambulance sped along the broad, palm-lined streets of San José. Through the windshield in front the boy saw the grilled ironwork of Spanish-type homes or lush green parks with winding paths, as they flashed by. At intervals brightly painted carts with large, wooden wheels drew across their path at intersections. The ambulance came to a screeching halt to allow the oxen pulling the vehicles to plod by. But at last, to Randy's intense relief, the ambulance safely came to a stop in a hospital entrance-way.

The two attendants quickly carried Louie into an examination room, and left before Randy could stammer his thanks. A pretty, olive-skinned nurse, who was apparently in charge, turned sympathetic eyes on Louie. Then, with a flash of white teeth, she spoke to Randy. *"Momentito, Señor."*

She was back a short while later with a handsome, white-haired man whom she introduced as Dr. Perez. The doctor shook hands with Randy and mentioned a call from Dr. Alvarez of Puntarenas. Then he turned to examine the patient. Presently he wheeled, speaking in a lowered tone to the nurse. She hurried out.

"Dr. Alvarez warned me that immediate surgery might be necessary, and he is right, Randy. I would like to delay if I could. You must have had a rough trip."

Thinking of the ambulance ride, Randy fervently agreed.

Two hospital orderlies now appeared. As they started to wheel Louie to the surgery, he cried, "Wait!" With an effort, he removed the Navajo bracelet from his wrist and held it out in a damp palm. "I want you to have this, Randy."

The boy was shaken by the suggestion. It seemed to imply that Louie did not believe he would survive the operation. "I—I can't take it, Louie!"

"I want you to have it," Louie insisted huskily. "For keeps."

The doctor saw the boy's hesitation. He gave a short nod that plainly said, "Take it. We can't delay!"

Randy's hand shook as he accepted the silver band. "Thanks, Louie. I'm sure everything will go all right."

There was an empty sensation in the boy's stomach as he watched the orderlies wheel Louie from the room. He glanced at the Navajo bracelet, which had never left Louie's wrist from the day he had bought it. Had he parted with it, his most prized possession, out of gratitude to Randy for helping him to reach the hospital in time? Or did Louie have grave doubts as to whether he'd live to wear the band again?

"I'll show you to the waiting room, *señor*," said the nurse, as the doctor followed the orderlies.

Randy looked with distaste at the skillfully wrought bracelet with its turquoise settings, and wished that Louie had never given it to him. Then he slipped it into his pocket, picked up the two sea bags and the now empty bucket and followed the girl into the corridor. His steps had somehow lost their spring.

CHAPTER TEN

Clues in the *Ripple's* Log

ALTHOUGH THERE were eight other people in the waiting room of the Chaqui Hospital, no one spoke to Randy, and he felt strangely alone. He grew more concerned about Louie as the minutes dragged by.

At length, he removed the Navajo bracelet from his pocket for want of something better to do, and studied its turquoise setting. He wondered what impulse had made Louie give it to him when the captain's son was so fond of the band.

The boy was still pondering this question when an elderly nurse, with plain, gold-rimmed glasses, entered the waiting room. "You're *Señor* Draper?"

"*Si, señora,*" said Randy, rising.

The woman smiled. "Your friend has just come from surgery," she informed him in Spanish. "He's in Room 109, which looks upon the garden."

Having had forebodings about the operation, Randy felt immensely relieved. "May I see him?" he asked eagerly.

"When he comes out of anaesthesia, yes. But while you wait, I would like some information for our records."

The nurse led the way to an office and began to question Randy. She made entries on a form as he answered. After obtaining what data she required, she accepted a deposit and gave the boy a receipt.

"I have my friend's bag," Randy explained.

"I'll have a *mozo* take it to his room. Please remain in the waiting room. Dr. Perez wishes to speak to you."

An orderly came for Louie's bag, but another half-hour passed before the doctor appeared. He smiled as he shook the boy's hand. "All is well, my young friend. Your *compañero* may leave in a week, if there are no complications."

"A week!" gasped Randy. "I don't think Captain Castignoni . . ."

"I am better able to judge such matters," broke in the doctor. "You have found a place to stay?"

Randy said he had not. The doctor wrote an address on a prescription pad, and tore off the page for Randy.

"You'll find El Conquistador modest but comfortable." Dr. Perez bowed slightly and shook Randy's hand again— frequent hand-shaking seemed to be the custom in Costa Rica.

The small, two-story hotel was on a palm-shaded street, only two blocks from the hospital. Randy registered and was shown to a room. He remained there only long enough to remove travel stains, before coming downstairs to the tiny dining-room.

It was almost seven when he signed the check for his meal. Walking to the desk, he asked how to call the Customs House in Puntarenas. The obliging desk clerk led Randy to a booth and put through the call.

"It's Randy," the boy said when he heard the captain's voice. "Louie came through his operation in fine shape, but the doctor won't let him leave for a week. Can't I return to the boat, instead of wasting my time here?"

"You are to stay with Louie until he can travel!" said Castignoni.

As he returned to the hospital, Randy wondered why the skipper had insisted that he stay with Louie rather than return to fishing. Louie was almost a man! In considering the matter, however, the boy concluded that Captain Castignoni was right. At home, Louie had left even minor decisions to his younger brother. He would be helpless by himself!

Upon reaching Room 109 of the hospital, Randy found Louie still stupefied by the anaesthetic. He dropped off to sleep shortly after the boy's arrival, and was still slumbering when a nurse came to tell Randy that all visitors must leave.

Randy returned in the morning. Louie, propped up with pillows, was eating a light breakfast.

"Why didn't you come sooner, Randy?"

The boy laughed. "I was here last night, Louie, but you didn't know me."

"Stay with me as much as you can," Louie pleaded. "I can't talk Spanish. I don't know what the nurses are saying."

Louie had always acted as though he considered himself superior to both Frank and Randy. His admission that he now needed the younger boy seemed rather odd to Randy.

Randy placed the Navajo bracelet on the bedspread. "Put it on, Louie."

"I meant for you to have it. I've been pretty rough on you and Frank. But when I was in a bad spot, you still helped out."

Randy laughed, lifted Louie's left arm and slipped the

silver band over his hand. A suggestion of a smile lighted Louie's dark face. "Thanks, Randy. I'd miss it."

"Why? Is it your lucky charm or something?"

"No." After a moment's hesitation Louie said slowly, "No one told me to buy it. I saw it, I liked it and I went into the shop to get it."

"Well . . . ?" asked Randy.

Louie made a helpless gesture. "I know. That's what most other people would do, isn't it? But not me! When I'm faced with a problem, I think of so many reasons why I should or shouldn't do a thing that I end up by not doing anything. This bracelet was an exception!"

The explanation seemed pointless to Randy until he realized that it provided a clue to Louie's character.

"Do you always have trouble deciding what to do?" he asked in amazement.

Louie's eyes dropped and he began to turn the bracelet. "I'm like Mama that way," he confessed at last.

"Your father said that your Grandfather Mazzanini met all problems in his home," observed Randy. "Maybe that's why your mother finds it hard to decide things for herself."

"If Mama had to decide anything, she'd get so rattled she could hardly remember her name," Louie admitted. "And when she went to pieces over some problem, I'd get fussed up, too. It got so that I couldn't trust my own judgment any more than Mama could. I'd run in circles, scream and shout —as the saying goes. Frank would see us both trying to make up our minds, and he'd suggest something. We'd usually be so relieved at having things taken out of our hands that we'd do what he advised, though it wasn't always the wisest course."

A feeling of excitement surged through Randy. "Were you sarcastic with Frank and me because we could decide what we wanted to do?"

Louie's expression of astonishment clearly showed that he had never before considered that possibility.

"Maybe I was jealous of you two; you were both so sure of yourselves." Louie paused, as if turning this new idea about in his mind. "After Frank started running things when Papa was away at sea, Mama consulted him about everything. She never asked my advice!"

"And because you were jealous," Randy sputtered indignantly, "you badgered Frank and me!"

"You two imagined you were pretty smart," Louie flared. "Remember the time you thought you could repair the carburetor? And the day you tried to save money by putting up the TV aerial that had blown down?"

"Frank and I made plenty of mistakes," Randy conceded. "The only way to escape that was to duck responsibility. The way you did in refusing to study navigation, or in steering the *Ripple* as poorly as you could."

Memory of the taunts he and Frank had taken from Louie had made the boy's voice rise in anger. A nurse now appeared to learn what was causing the disturbance.

"You must not excite the patient!" she declared reprovingly.

Observing how tired Louie looked, Randy was ashamed of his outburst.

"I'm sorry, Louie," he said apologetically. "I'll go and let you rest."

He was turning toward the door when Louie called, *"Randy!"*

The boy wheeled in surprise.

"I'm the one who should say I'm sorry. But I never understood before why I felt like nagging you and Frank. Now that I realize what's behind it . . ." He made a vague, uncertain gesture. "Well, I won't take out my own faults on you any longer. I'm going to—to buy some more Navajo bracelets."

Randy grasped the other's meaning. Louie meant that he'd try to reach his own decisions, maybe even take more responsibility. But the boy had little faith that such a right-about-face would last. However sincere Louie's intentions might be, Randy saw small likelihood that the captain's son would change.

When Randy returned to the hospital at noon, however, Louie's smile was so cheerful that he reminded the boy of Frank.

"This Costa Rican mountain coffee is really tops. Can I have the nurse bring you a cup?"

Randy's jaw dropped in astonishment.

"You don't believe I can change, do you?" Louie asked with a grin, and pressed the bell. When a nurse appeared, he said, "Randy, will you . . . ?" And then an oddly determined expression came over Louie's face. "No! Tell *me* how to ask for coffee."

Randy suppressed a smile. *"Un café con leche."*

Slowly Louie repeated the phrase. The nurse smiled and

disappeared. Louie's eyes lighted triumphantly when the nurse returned with a cup of coffee and a small pitcher of milk for Randy.

The boy's suspicion that Louie would find it difficult to mend his ways was nevertheless well founded. While they talked his lips would sometimes curl with the contemptuous sneer that had become habitual with him. Or his voice would take on an acid note. But he would catch himself, flushing with annoyance, and say angrily, "I won't be like that!"

Louie's ground-floor room looked out upon the attractive hospital grounds, and as Randy visited, he noticed a middle-aged patient hobbling slowly along the winding path. The man was large and fair-haired, and dressed in well-worn dungarees.

"I've seen that fellow before," Louie cried abruptly.

Randy went to the window. The man was a complete stranger to him. "Reminds you of Freshwater, doesn't he?"

"A little. And I have a hunch he's a fisherman, too."

"Shall I ask him?" Randy inquired, not expecting an affirmative reply.

"Why don't you?" said Louie. "He might be glad to find someone here who speaks his own tongue."

The man had disappeared when Randy reached the garden. After a short search, however, the boy found him sitting on a shaded bench. A contagious good humor lighted the stranger's pale-blue eyes.

"You look American to me," he said jovially. "Come and sit down."

Randy dropped onto the bench. "I'm Randy Draper of San

Diego, making my first cruise on the *Ripple.*"

"Joe Castignoni's boat," observed the man. "I know Joe, but I'm better acquainted with his brother Vittorio." He put out a large, freckled hand to grip the boy's. "Glad to find another tuna fisherman here, Randy. My name's Gunnison— Axel Gunnison. You don't look like an invalid to me."

"No, I came with Louie Castignoni. He had his appendix removed."

"What a small world! I met Louie several times on his uncle's boat. I sailed on the *Westwind* for four years. But when my brother and I had a chance to buy the clipper *Ocean Belle*, I transferred to her. Lucky thing I did, too. Vittorio Castignoni's boat was lost several months later."

Gunnison explained how a scratch on his leg had become infected, making it necessary to leave the *Ocean Belle* at Puntarenas and come to San José for an operation. His surgeon was the same Dr. Perez who had operated on Louie.

"Couldn't have found a better surgeon back home," said Gunnison, slapping his leg. "I'm not high-stepping yet, but I'll be able to board the *Belle* when she returns to Puntarenas a week from now."

"My friend Frank Castignoni was on the *Westwind*," Randy said soberly. "Have you any idea what happened to her?"

Axel Gunnison shook his head. "I could tell you plenty about Old Vittorio, though. What a character! He believed in many of the Old World superstitions. When the *Westwind* was built, for example, he placed a new silver dollar at the base of the mast to bring the boat good luck. Some older tuna

· 178 ·

fishermen believe that if you mount a set of antlers on the mast, any bad wishes directed at the boat will be deflected back to the ill-wisher from the points of the horns. So Old Vittorio nailed up the whole head and antlers of a deer one of his men had shot, thinking that would give him extra protection, I guess. The deer head got to smelling so bad that one night several of us climbed the mast and chucked it overboard."

Gunnison laughed as another memory returned to mind.

"Vittorio followed many other Old World customs. On the *Westwind's* maiden voyage he insisted that the first tuna caught must be released. There's an ancient belief that the fish will swim away and tell other fish that there are kind men on the boat. Yellowfins and skipjacks are supposed to be so grateful for the good treatment that they'll flock to such a boat to be caught. Vittorio would also allow the first fish taken after every overhaul to go free. He believed that as long as he paid attention to his Old World customs, he'd have big hauls. But the real explanation of that was in his ability to find tuna."

"He never got over the thrifty habits he learned in Italy, either," observed Randy. "He'd collect oil drums for the deposits they'd bring."

"I could tell you something about that," said Gunnison, chuckling. "On our first cruise with the *Ocean Belle,* the barometer started to drop as we reached the southern Costa Rican coast. My brother Sverre was afraid that with the glass showing low pressure, we might have a storm. So we ducked into the Gulf of Dulce. Few vessels put in there because of the sheer cliffs and the deep water. But we found an anchorage under a precipice, that would shelter us from any winds that might blow. And we made use of the lost time to transfer twenty barrels of Diesel oil to our fuel tanks. We planned to drop the empty drums later, after we were out at sea. But when the *Westwind* appeared and let go her hook near us, I thought of another idea.

"I told Sverre about Vittorio's habit of picking up marine salvage. I said we might sell Vittorio our oil drums and later, in San Diego, josh him about buying junk we'd intended to cast overboard. My brother didn't think Vittorio would bite. When he rowed over to the *Westwind* and offered the drums for a dollar and a half each, however, Castignoni snapped at the offer because he'd make more than fifty per cent. He even sent over his net skiff to collect our drums."

The humor died from Gunnison's face. "We never had a chance to twit Vittorio about our prank, though. By the time we reached San Diego, all radio contact had been lost with the *Westwind*."

"Then you saw her just before she sailed to the Gulf of Panama, Mr. Gunnison?" Randy asked.

The big fisherman nodded. "I guess we were the last men to speak with her crew. We visited back and forth during the two days the storm held us in the Gulf of Dulce. When we put to sea again the *Westwind* sailed southward, while we decided to try our luck to the north."

"It must have been only a few days later that Frank Castignoni called me by radiophone from the Gulf of Panama. Do you suppose his uncle might have sailed from there to the

Galápagos Islands?"

"My brother and I have discussed that," admitted Gunnison. "Vittorio had taken some tuna before he sailed southward, though, and the skipper with a partial load usually tries to fill his wells by sailing in the direction of his home port. Panama, of course, was not far out of his way, but the Galápagos would be."

"But perhaps Captain Vittorio was scouting out the fishing possibilities of the islands for his next cruise," suggested Randy.

"That could be," conceded the big fisherman. "But in the weeks that have passed since his boat disappeared, many clippers have visited the Galápagos. Most of them sailed directly from San Diego or San Pedro, taking both bait and tuna at the islands. In scouting for fish, the crews would hardly miss any vessel as large as the *Westwind*."

Randy was not convinced. While studying the Galápagos chart, he had learned that there were several hundred islands in the group, some rather large and others scarcely more than gigantic rocks. He doubted that the waters of the archipelago could have been fully explored by tuna boats since the time of the *Westwind's* disappearance.

"Would there be any way to learn whether Captain Vittorio did visit the islands?" Randy asked after a thoughtful pause.

Gunnison shook his head. "He didn't report any such plans to the Italo-American Cannery or to anyone else, so far as I've heard. There's a bare chance he might have confided in his brother. Joe and Vittorio talked by radiophone every night or so."

"Would my skipper have a record of their conversations?" Randy asked excitedly.

"He might have made entries in his log," Gunnison answered.

A "log," the boy knew, was a record book every captain was required to keep. Into it went the daily happenings of a voyage: the time a vessel sailed or passed important landmarks, the names of crew members signed on or discharged, how many tuna were caught, what weather conditions were encountered, the report of damage to a boat, or the injuries suffered and the treatment given fishermen when accidents occurred. Almost anything concerning the boat or her crew might go into a log.

Gunnison chuckled. "When I was the *Westwind's* helmsman, I used to overhear Vittorio's long-winded radio conversations with his brother. He'd tell Joe if he picked up a skiff that could be repaired, or even mention a bunch of oil drums he'd salvaged."

"Would *that* go into our log?" Randy asked eagerly.

The big fisherman had a puzzled look. "What makes you ask?"

"Well, the *Westwind* took aboard thirty oil-drums at Almejas Bay, and you say that you sold her twenty more."

"I'd be willing to bet she had twice that many, Randy. Vittorio never passed up any oil barrels in good enough shape to bring a refund. I have a hunch that he might have picked up some other drums while we waited out the storm in the Gulf of Dulce."

· 182 ·

"One hundred oil-drums!" gasped Randy. "Were the caps screwed on?"

"The ones we sold Vittorio had screw caps, yes. But what are you driving at, boy?"

"Mr. Gunnison," Randy exclaimed, "how could a boat with a hundred air-tight oil drums sink? She'd have too much buoyancy, wouldn't she?"

Gunnison's jaw dropped; then he gave a low whistle.

"Son, you have something there! I can recall two sinking tuna boats that were towed back safely to San Diego by sea-going tugs after marine salvors filled all spaces below decks with empty oil barrels. And they were kept afloat for hundreds of miles!"

Suddenly the excitement died in Randy. "But we don't know for sure that the *Westwind* carried more than fifty empty drums!"

"Not unless Joe Castignoni recorded others in his log."

"Oh, I forgot!" exclaimed Randy suddenly, springing up. "Louie wanted to see you!"

That evening Randy called Captain Castignoni at the Puntarenas Customs House. He reported Louie's favorable progress.

"That's fine!" the skipper cried heartily. "We took several tons of tuna just outside the gulf today. Now that Louie is out of danger, we may stay out longer—if we can find any schools. So don't be disturbed if I'm not here when you call tomorrow night."

"Captain," the boy said quickly, "did you ever record the

wireless conversations with your brother?"

"At times I'd jot down a line or so in the log."

"Were there any entries about oil drums taken aboard on the *Westwind's* last cruise?"

The captain's voice was noticeably cool: "I can't recall."

"Is the log used then aboard the *Ripple*, sir?"

"It is," said the skipper brusquely.

Realizing that the subject was distasteful to Captain Castignoni, Randy said good-by and hung up. Stepping from the booth, he was confronted by a handsome young Costa Rican.

"You are *Señor* Draper?" he asked in surprise. "I expected someone older. I am *Señor* García, a reporter from *El San José Diario*. Would you tell me about the friend you accompanied to the hospital and of your experiences at sea?"

One of the nurses, Randy suspected, had spoken to the reporter about the young Americans. The boy hesitated, but could think of no reason for refusing to answer *Señor* García's questions. He described the hurried trip to the capital with Louie. And when the reporter asked about his tuna-fishing experiences, Randy told briefly of his unpleasant days on a hatch cover, of his escape from a shark and of his scouting flights with Steve Vardon.

At last, with a dazzling smile, *Señor* García closed his notebook. "This will give me a nice little story. Thank you, *Señor.*"

Two days later the "nice little story" occupied two full columns of the *Diario*. Randy took a copy of the paper to the hospital. He and Louie were amused by the somewhat

florid style, and by several inaccuracies, which were ac-
counted for by the reporter's ignorance of how tuna were
caught.

Randy later mailed the account to his mother, and then
forgot the matter—though not for long.

Louie was able to walk a few steps on the second day
after his operation. The following day, and every afternoon
thereafter the doctor allowed Randy to rent a car and driver
and take the patient on an hour's drive around the city. San
José was very attractive, with its National Theatre, where
traveling opera companies made appearances, its spacious
streets and its numerous parks, brilliant with flowering trees
and shrubs.

Yet Randy begrudged every moment he was obliged to
remain in the capital. He was impatient to discover what
light the *Ripple's* log might shed upon the mysterious disappearance of the clipper *Westwind.*

And one morning, to the boy's great relief, Dr. Perez removed Louie's dressings and stitches and said that he might
leave. Randy quickly settled his accounts with the doctor and
the hospital, and checked out of the small hotel where he
was staying.

Although Louie had shown in many small ways that he
was trying hard to make a change for the better, Randy was
surprised, upon reaching the station, to hear Louie ask if he
might buy the tickets.

"I've got to learn some time," he said, flushing.

Randy knew that the captain's son had picked up a few
words of Spanish in the hospital, but he doubted if Louie's

grasp of the language was equal to the test. Thinking the experience might be good for Louie, however, Randy said, "Go ahead."

By use of gestures and his limited Spanish, Louie finally purchased two tickets. His delight at his success, however, was short-lived. The parlor-car conductor refused them admittance, and they had to walk back to the day coach and take their places on the hard wooden seats.

"I should have let you buy the tickets," said Louie in disappointment.

"You saved us money," said Randy cheerfuly. "This is all right."

Randy was not sure they would find the *Ripple* at Puntarenas. But after a short walk with their sea bags, he saw her moored where they had left her.

Fishermen shouted when they saw the pair making their way along the wharf. Captain Castignoni hurried down from the bridge as they climbed aboard. "How do you feel, Louie?" he asked anxiously.

"All right, Papa. Just a little tired from the train ride."

"You lie down. You rest a little. You want something to eat?"

"Not right now," said Louie.

When Louie disappeared into his room, Randy followed the captain to the bridge. He handed the skipper an itemized list of his expenses and an envelope holding what money remained.

Castignoni scanned the list and said, "Fine! Fine, Randy! I guess this was not too pleasant for you, eh?"

"Louie and I hit it off great now, sir." And then he spoke of the matter that had haunted him for days. "Could I see that log, Captain?"

The muscles tightened around the skipper's mouth. In silence he strode into his room and brought out a thin volume, bound in red cloth.

"I can't imagine why you should want this," he said stiffly, and walked over to pull the bell cord.

The Diesels were humming when Randy went below. Finding the galley deserted, he laid the log on the table. The first entries concerned the testing of engines, lights and whistle preparatory to leaving San Diego. Quickly he turned the pages until he came upon a notation made eight days after the *Ripple* had put to sea. It read:

Talked with Vittorio at 8:37 p. m. He says fishing is poor.

Randy ran on. There were other references to radio conversations between the captain and his brother, but they were either obscure or mentioned only the weather or the poor fishing conditions the *Westwind* was encountering. Then, on June 21, there was a significant entry:

Talked with Vittorio 9:01 p. m. when he was leaving Port Angeles. He had trouble convincing Mexican officials he'd come into port to pump water from port wells to correct a slight list. Says he picked up sixteen oil drums. Probably will cost him more to transport than they'll bring in refunds! We were so poor as kids in Italy that Vittorio can't bear any waste.

Several days later there was another entry that interested Randy:

Reached Vittorio at Magdalena Bay, 8:18 p. m. Says he can't find bait, and will try Almejas. He took aboard fourteen oil drums!

Vittorio Castignoni reported from Almejas Bay a few days later that anchovettas were plentiful, and that he had recovered thirty oil drums left on the beach by two San Diego clippers.

Other entries showed that the *Ripple* and the *Westwind* were in almost daily radio contact as they sailed southward. Most of these entries concerned fishing conditions, however, so the boy skipped rapidly over them.

Then he came upon an entry that he studied thoughtfully. It read:

Vittorio has taken shelter in Gulf of Dulce due to storm. Says he's taken half a load in small catches and is thinking of trying the Galápagos if hauls continue to be poor. He bought twenty oil-barrels from Ocean Belle—*how the boys must have enjoyed their joke!*

Several lines further down the captain had jotted down an odd report from his brother. Vittorio Castignoni, after taking forty tons of yellowfins, had decided not to visit the Galápagos. And while a dead calm prevailed in the Gulf of Panama, he had sent a skiff ashore to find hardwood he hoped to make into a chair. The crew had returned not only with the wood but with a load of oil drums that had recently drifted ashore!

There were notations indicating that Joe Castignoni had tried to reach his brother in the Gulf of Panama. One seemed to Randy to have special significance, for it ran:

Can't reach Vittorio—static bad.

For six consecutive days that comment appeared in the log. And on the seventh, the captain had written:

Storm continuing in Gulf of Panama, according to reports. I'm worried about Vittorio and Frank. Called cannery. But they've heard nothing from Westwind *all this week.*

The captain's next entry concerned a radio call to Panama to request that Coast Guard planes look for his brother's boat. Five days later he recorded, in a heavy hand, the unhappy outcome of that appeal:

Coast Guard reports that all efforts to find Westwind *have failed. They have abandoned search. I know what this means, but I find it hard to accept the truth.*

Randy stared at the plainly expressed but moving words for several minutes. Then, his lips tightening, he reached for the pad on which the cook planned his menus and began to jot down the number of oil drums that Vittorio Castignoni had reported finding.

When he totaled these figures, he was astonished to discover that the *Westwind* had had 121 oil drums aboard when she disappeared.

Randy hurried up to the bridge with the sheet of figures and the log. He had heard the clipper stop, minutes earlier, to drop her pilot. Now he saw that she was approaching the entrance of the Gulf of Nicoya. Steve was at the wheel, and Joe Castignoni stood at the window.

"Captain!" the boy cried breathlessly. "The *Westwind* must have sailed to the Galápagos, and she might still be afloat. . . ."

The skipper wheeled about, his face dark with anger. "I must ask you *never* to mention that boat again!" he said sternly.

Randy's eyes flooded. He could well understand the captain's desire to forget the tragic loss he had suffered when his brother's boat had vanished. But now Randy had uncovered evidence that the *Westwind* might yet be adrift—her crew alive—and he could not speak!

There was a painful lump in the boy's throat as he turned into the captain's room and laid the log on the chart table. Then, hastily, he left the bridge.

CHAPTER ELEVEN

Hazards for the Helmsman

RANDY SAT with legs dangling from a bait tank; staring bleakly off to port. Though he watched the dark shadows of drifting clouds flowing across Costa Rica's coastal mountains, his mind was on the *Westwind*.

Even if the missing clipper had struck a rock and filled with water, he thought, she must still be a floating derelict. The air confined in the 121 oil drums she carried should prevent her from sinking much below her decks. Yet there were unanswered questions. Where was the boat? Why had no one heard from her crew? Randy could think of but one plausible explanation. The men must be marooned on an island, possibly one of the remote isles of the Galápagos.

He would never know for certain whether he was right unless he could persuade Captain Castignoni to visit the islands. The skipper was not likely to do that unless Randy presented the evidence he had discovered in the log. And he was forbidden to discuss that!

Hearing sounds, he turned and saw Steve climbing the bait tank ladder.

"Help me remove the tarp from my plane, Randy."

Randy glanced at the heaving seas. "Isn't it too rough to take off?"

"Maybe I'll be piloting a bunch of flying bolts before I

can get her into the air," said Steve cheerily. "But the Old Man says we've already lost too much time this trip."

They clambered up onto the wooden canopy, rolled back the tarpaulin and lashed it securely at one side.

"May I go along, Steve?"

"Look at those swells—and decide for yourself, Randy."

Steve checked the plane with great care, and then revved it up for a quarter-hour before sending a fisherman to call the chief engineer. The vessel hove to presently, McDowd swung the hydroplane over the side and it landed with a splash.

Randy freed the winch hooks and slipped back into his seat.

Steve opened the throttle. The plane roared and shook, pounding along heavily in the big swells. Sheets of spray lashed pontoons and windows. Then at last the little plane was wobbling in a laboring climb.

"Now let's find tuna," Steve yelled.

He banked the monoplane, and they flew in ever-widening circles around the clipper. Finding no schools of fish near the boat, Steve leveled out and buzzed southward. They had flown perhaps fifteen miles on a straight course when the pilot suddenly waggled the wings and began to dive.

Far ahead of the plane Randy made out a long line of porpoises, leaping and splashing. To the south of the playful mammals, for a distance of nearly three miles, the disturbed sea glinted with brief flashes.

"Could a school of tuna be that large!" Randy shouted.

"They come larger," answered Steve. "But I've never

seen a bigger one."

He switched on the short-wave radio and called the *Ripple*. Joe Castignoni's voice soon filtered through the loudspeaker.

"That you, Steve? Over."

"Remember that school you once hit off Acapulco, Joe? I have one that ought to be its equal. Over."

The captain's voice shook with excitement. "What course, Steve?"

"Straight south. I'm staying here till I run out of gas. I don't want to lose this one! That's all."

Steve skimmed low to get a better idea of the school's size; then he climbed and leveled out. Reducing speed to conserve gas, he began to circle.

"Hope it isn't a school that won't take lures or bait," he shouted.

"The sea is getting mighty rough," Randy observed.

It seemed a long time to the boy before the *Ripple* drew near the northward-moving tuna. Steve pushed the plane's nose forward. Presently they were skimming over the tops of the crested swells. Randy's heart stood still as Steve set the craft down in a trough. The little plane struck with a jarring impact, bounded and then hit a second time with a loud *thwack*.

Spray washed over fuselage and windows as they taxied forward, rolling far over on a wing. The boy clenched his teeth in expectation of a crash and a possible explosion. But it never came. The hydroplane righted itself; the seas no longer broke around them. Timing his landing perfectly,

Steve had brought the craft in safely on the clipper's lee side.

He shut off the ignition and turned to grin at his passenger. "Another quarter-hour, and we'd have had trouble landing."

Randy nodded speechlessly.

Still shaking, he climbed out to secure the winch hooks. The plane was quickly lifted onto her chocks. As several fishermen finished lashing it in place, someone shouted that the vessel was surrounded by tuna.

Randy dropped to the deck and joined the others at the rail. The sea swarmed with yellowfins—great fish that must weigh nearly a hundred pounds.

"Three-polers!" announced Freshwater. "Where's Louie?"

"He shouldn't be fishing yet," said Randy, starting at a run for their three-pole rig. "Steve will have to be our third man."

Trouble developed when fishing began. The heavy rolling of the vessel plunged the men to their waists or deeper in the sea. Under such conditions it was difficult for three men to time their strikes together. One or more of the fishermen was likely to be fighting to maintain his balance at the moment a yellowfin charged the squid. Every so often there would be a wail as a pole snapped. And, at other times, a chorus of yells would be heard as entire rigs were carried away.

Somewhat offsetting these difficulties was the eagerness of the fish. They leaped half-clear of the water to seize the chums Doc Bernedetto cast beyond the rack. They snatched squids as they struck the water. When they felt the sudden tension of the barbless hooks, the big tunas struggled with fury, tails whipping while they were being swung aboard. Steadily the catch piled up between the rail and the bait tank.

By sundown sharks had become so numerous and the vessel rolled so wildly that everyone was grateful to see the day end.

"The biggest school I've seen in years—and to find it when the swells are running like this," lamented the captain. "We've hardly taken ten tons of fish."

"That's how it goes," said Steve with a bitterness unusual for him. "The seas might moderate by morning, but I doubt it."

Throughout the night the *Ripple* sailed northward, while off her starboard side the water glowed with the prosphorescence stirred up by the moving school of fish. Whenever it appeared that the fish might outdistance the boat, Doc Bernedetto drew yellowfins to the clipper by casting off scoop after scoop of anchovettas.

In the morning the sea still teemed with fish, but the men faced appalling conditions. The iron rack vanished with every port roll. And no sooner had fishing begun than sharks commenced to make swift, slashing attacks. They seized yellowfins taking the feathered jigs, and often snapped off half of a fish as it was being swung aboard.

The men had even more difficulty in maintaining balance and in achieving teamwork than on the previous day. This lack of coördination resulted in so many cracked and shattered poles that a recess had to be called at midday. All polished bamboo on the boat was then made up into new outfits.

Twenty hard-earned tons of fish were boated by the time the sun set, but at a price that left every man exhausted.

Chumming was continued during the night to hold at least a portion of the school. But in the morning Randy wondered if it had been worth the effort. The boat swung with such abandon that he could hardly walk the deck.

Nevertheless, the men grimly returned to the racks. After Puccinelli and the captain narrowly escaped being swept overboard, however, the discouraged teams gave more thought to safety than to fishing. Tuna were released by quick downstrokes of the poles whenever men feared for their footing.

The skipper saw that his crew had lost heart. At noon he ordered fishing racks raised, and set sail for Puntarenas.

Randy helped stow away the five tons of tuna taken that morning, then went to change into dry clothing. He found Louie dressing.

"Jack Lucca and I are going to have a look at the town," he said good naturedly. "Hop into shore duds if you'd like to come along."

Randy had misgivings, but he said, "I'll hurry. We'll soon be in."

To the boy's surprise, it was a pleasant excursion. Louie took the lead in venturing into the stores and small shops of the town. And when he saw Randy debating over a creamer and sugar bowl wrought by Mexican tinsmiths, he surprised his companions by buying the set and presenting it to the boy as a gift for his mother.

Jack Lucca's brows rose in amazement, and later he whispered to Randy, "What's happened to Louie? He was never like this!"

The *Ripple* remained in port for two days. With the skies clearing then, she sailed northward in search of tuna. A wind, cold for those latitudes, was soon raising heavy seas. By late afternoon conditions were so severe that the clipper was obliged to turn back.

For the first time on the cruise, Randy was hurled from his upper bunk by the violent wallowing of the boat. Protected by his blankets, he was only shaken up. Yet he decided to lay where he had fallen rather than risk injury by returning to his bed.

Some time later he was aroused from a sound sleep by a hand on his arm. "Come quick, Randy," said a voice he recognized as the captain's.

Scrambling from his blankets, he followed the skipper. They lurched in zigzags, making their way forward along the rolling deck. Off to port greenish-blue flashes of sea fire revealed the great height of the tumbling swells.

The captain stopped at the foot of the ladder and leaned over a prone figure. It was the navigator! His eyes were closed and there was a streak of blood across his forehead.

"What—what happened, sir?" Randy faltered.

"I don't know exactly," said Castignoni. "Steve called me at the end of my watch, and after he left the bridge I heard a *thump*. I set the Iron Mike and stepped out to see what was wrong. I found Steve lying here. Must have been thrown from the ladder."

"I hope he's not badly hurt, Captain."

"So do I! . . . Go topside and stand watch while I find someone to help me carry him to his room."

"What course, sir?"

"Leave the clipper on automatic pilot. Just stand by, and sound the bell if you see anything ahead."

Randy hurried up to the bridge. He had never stood a solitary watch when the boat was under way. It made him uneasy to do so on such a night. The stars were hidden by a heavy overcast. Wind drove briny spray across the darkened sea. He could make out nothing ahead save the ghostly sparkles of phosphorescence.

He stood at the window, staring anxiously into the mirk, while the automatic pilot steered the vessel. He winced as the clipper buried her bow into big swells a helmsman might have avoided. He wished he could take the wheel to save the boat this punishment. Yet he dared not disregard the skipper's orders.

As he stared into the gloom, he recalled a story his father had told of a tuna clipper that had met disaster on such a night. She was on automatic pilot and stormy conditions prevented the man on watch from seeing an oil tanker bearing down on the vessel—until it was too late. There was a thunderous clash and screech of steel as the tanker ripped through the well deck. Only six fishermen were rescued after the tuna boat sank. . . .

Minutes dragged by before Randy heard heavy footsteps.

Freshwater burst into the wheelhouse and dashed into the captain's room. He pulled open the drawers that held the medical supplies.

"When will the skipper be back, Freshwater?"

"Carry on a while longer, Randy. Joe hasn't brought Steve around yet."

Freshwater gathered up a roll of adhesive tape and another of gauze, and hurried out.

Randy resigned himself to a long vigil.

He was startled, some time later, to hear a faint booming of breakers above the seething and clashing of the seas. Opening a window to hear better, he listened for several minutes without catching any sounds other than the roar of the swells and the creaking of the vessel. Then once more he detected a booming and cracking reminiscent of breakers pounding rocky cliffs.

It was not the sound itself but the direction from which it came that caused the boy's muscles to tighten with alarm. The cannonading seemed to come from directly ahead of the *Ripple!*

Randy grasped the bell cord, then hesitated. The captain would be furious if he were called from his patient without good reason.

Randy hurried into the skipper's room and switched on the light above the chart table. From the last position marked on the chart, he traced the vessel's probable southward course. The boat must be drawing near Cabo Blanco, the great headland indicated at the western approach of the Gulf of Nicoya. If Captain Castignoni had shaped their course to sail to the westward of the cape, breakers might well be heard off to port. But that was not the direction from which the sounds were coming!

Randy ran back to the window and tried to locate the Isla Blanca Light. It stood on a 100-foot iron framework on the summit of the bare, rocky isle lying to the west of the cape. Either it was hidden by Cabo Blanco or screened in mists, for he could not see it. The booming of breakers, however, was clearly audible. And the sounds, he was certain, came from the southward.

Randy dashed back to the captain's room for another look at the chart. It showed soundings of only forty fathoms off the northeastern part of the cape; beneath the headland the water must shoal to even lesser depths. Rocks might be found in these shallows, and where there were rocks there could be breakers. But it worried him that there were none large enough to be shown on the chart, either to the northeast or off the seaward side of the cape.

What he heard must be the seas crashing against Cabo Blanco!

Greatly alarmed now, he ran forward to confirm his suspicion that the roaring and booming came from the southward. It did, indeed! A thunderous clashing from that direction drowned out every other sound.

Randy started toward the bell, then froze as the booming beyond the bow grew deafening. The captain could never reach the bridge in time to avert disaster!

The boy knew it was a serious matter to disobey a master's orders. But if he didn't do so, the vessel would rush on to her destruction.

His hand shook as he released the automatic pilot. Moments later he shoved the engine-room telegraph to *Slow;* then, after a short interval, to *Stop.* The bombardment of the seas against rocky cliffs now filled the wheelhouse with a clamorous din. Swiftly Randy took the final step, pushing the telegraph lever to *Reverse.*

The vessel shuddered, her screw battling momentum. In the grip of these opposing forces, the *Ripple* continued her forward motion several seconds longer. The propeller had not yet gained the upper hand when Randy saw the livid flash of breaking seas ahead.

A moment more—and the clipper struck the shelving shore! She was churning water then, had almost come to a stop. The impact scarcely jarred her.

It seemed ages to Randy, standing at the wheel, before the boat, trembling violently, began to back off the cliffs. Flying mists quickly screened the breakers from view.

The door was flung back. Captain Castignoni strode to the open window. He stood for some time listening to the cracking seas to the southward.

Randy's nerves quivered while he waited for the skipper to turn and upbraid him for disregarding orders. But Joe Castignoni gave no clue to his intentions; he appeared lost in thought.

At last Randy was unable to bear the suspense any longer. "D-do you want to take the wheel, sir?"

"I didn't say so." Castignoni's voice was milder than usual, and his words were followed by a short, dry laugh.

"Are you planning to back all the way to San Diego?"

"N-no, sir. I thought you'd want to take over."

"Don't see why I should. Can you find your way around the cape?"

"Yes, sir."

"Then do so."

Randy brought the vessel drifting to a stop before he pushed the telegraph lever to *Slow*. And not until he had swung the wheel to turn the clipper out to sea did he telegraph for *Full Speed Ahead*.

The recent scare made him overly cautious. He continued on a westerly course until he could distinguish the dim glow of the Isla Blanca Light through the mists. Then he swung southward, sailing well past the cape and Isla Blanca before turning through the broad entrance of the Gulf of Nicoya.

Randy was sure the captain would relieve him then. He had never been permitted to sail into a bay or a cove. But the skipper gave no sign that he meant to take over.

"I've never done such a thing before!" Castignoni said abruptly. "In my hurry to reach Steve, I must have made an error in setting the Iron Mike. Good thing you had the sense to take over in time!"

Feeling relieved that the skipper wasn't angry because of what he had done, Randy asked, "How is Steve, Captain?"

"Conscious now. I was afraid he had a fractured skull. But he believes he'll be all right."

Then, to Randy's astonishment, the captain himself brought up the subject he had sternly requested the boy never again to mention.

"What did you mean by your statement that the *Westwind* might still be afloat? What makes you believe that, Randy?"

"Why—because she could hardly sink, sir."

"*Could hardly sink!*" repeated the captain in amazement. "What do you mean by that? Every vessel can go to the bottom!"

"That's true, Captain," said Randy. "But the *Westwind* would have an awful difficult time doing it."

CHAPTER TWELVE

The Gentlemen from Nicaragua

CAPTAIN CASTIGNONI's dark eyes narrowed as though he imagined that Randy harbored some boyish notion unworthy of a mariner's serious thought. With an effort, however, he controlled his irritation.

"Any helmsman who saves my boat has the right to say his say," he declared. "What makes you believe the *Westwind* would have a hard time sinking?"

"Because she had 121 oil drums aboard, sir," said Randy.

The skipper understood instantly what that meant in providing artificial buoyancy. His eyes widened. His jaw sagged in astonishment.

"What makes you think so?" he asked sharply.

About to speak, Randy caught sight of two steadily burning lights, set several hundred yards apart. Despite the darkness, he could make out the silhouettes of the wooded isles on which these post lights stood.

"Shall I pass between the lights, sir?"

Momentarily the captain glanced from the window, "Yes, yes," he said impatiently. "Now, how do you know there were that many oil drums on my brother's boat?"

The boy spoke of the clues he had gathered from Hal Lassman and Axel Gunnison. "I verified their statements in the ship's log," Randy added. "There I discovered that your brother recovered other oil barrels—121 in all."

A faint smile flickered over the captain's hawklike face. "I can hardly dispute my own figures, can I?" He began to pace the wheelhouse, speaking rapidly, "My brother believed waste led to want. In my opinion, he carried this belief to extremes. It amused me to jot in my log the salvage he collected and reported to me in our wireless talks. But I did not always do so. Vittorio must have picked up more oil drums than are shown in the log."

Excitement seized Joe Castignoni as he grasped the significance of the air-tight barrels stowed beneath the *Westwind's* deck. His dark eyes were ablaze, his strong hands moved in quick, nervous gestures.

"You're right, Randy!" he cried, after pondering the matter more fully. "How could a boat with so much buoyancy sink? More than one tuna captain has saved his boat by buying oil drums to keep her afloat until he could reach port."

"The *Westwind* may have struck a rock, Captain," Randy suggested.

"Quite possible," agreed Castignoni. "But even if she filled with water and settled till her decks were awash, Vittorio and his crew could still launch skiffs—unless their small boats had been smashed in a storm."

"Frank called me from the Gulf of Panama," Randy went on. "Everyone took it for granted that your brother sailed northward a short time later and was caught by the storm that swept over the gulf. But I don't believe the *Westwind* was anywhere near the Central American coast at that time."

"What makes you think that?"

"Well, if your brother's clipper was as buoyant as we think, she'd wash ashore and be reported by natives. Or she'd be adrift, maybe partly submerged, and be reported as a derelict by a coasting boat. In either case, the crew could reach the mainland in skiffs."

"Not in a storm, Randy. They might have been wrecked on rocks or small islands."

"Yes, sir. But even if that happened, they could gather driftwood, build a raft and reach the coast during the first calm."

"Assuming you're right," said the captain. "Where does this lead?"

"It must mean the *Westwind* was not off the Central American coast when she sank, Captain!"

Castignoni frowned. "Then where was she, eh?"

"I think she sailed from the Gulf of Panama to the Galápagos Islands, sir." Seeing the skepticism in the skipper's face, the boy hurried on: "If the *Westwind* were disabled there, trade winds would blow her across the Pacific. She might fetch up on one of the South Sea islands, as the *Kon-Tiki* did, before she was sighted. And if her crew reached one of the uninhabited islands of the Galápagos group after the ship was damaged, no one might hear from them. The swift currents in the islands would make it too dangerous for the men to start out again to try to reach a populated island.

They might be carried westward into the Pacific if they tried it."

The glow faded from Castignoni's brown face. "You have a lively imagination, Randy. But my brother gave up the idea of sailing to the Galápagos Islands."

"Perhaps he changed his mind, sir."

"That's possible," said the captain without conviction. "However, if my brother did reconsider, there's not much chance that he or any of his crew are now alive. The American Tuna Boat Association alerted its members immediately after the *Westwind* was reported missing. Every captain visiting the Galápagos has searched for her crew when fishing there."

"There are hundreds of islands in the group," Randy faltered. "If the searching boats overlooked just one—the one on which the *Westwind's* crew is marooned . . ."

"I'll consider what you've said," declared Castignoni, in the tone of a man dismissing a distasteful subject.

Except for an occasional glance from the window, the captain had not concerned himself with navigation for many minutes. Randy had steered the vessel through the islands of the Gulf of Nicoya by memory alone. But now he was relieved to see the red and green lights of the government launch moving swiftly toward the *Ripple*. He hove to in order to allow the small boat to come alongside.

Joe Castignoni left the bridge to greet the four Costa Rican officers who came aboard. They had cleared the clipper only that morning, so three of their number quickly concluded their business and returned to the launch. The pilot came forward with the captain.

"Better sack in, Randy," Castignoni advised, as he stepped onto the bridge. "You've done a good night's work."

Before he went to the galley for breakfast the following morning, Randy visited the navigator's room. Steve Vardon was bolstered up with pillows. The icebag tied around his swollen head gave him such a comical appearance that Randy had difficulty smothering his mirth.

"I got the idea from a ladies' fashion magazine," Steve said ruefully. He winced and closed his eyes. "*Wow!* I have a headache big enough for a whale!"

The room suddenly darkened. The boy turned and saw the captain standing in the doorway.

"Hurry through your breakfast, Randy," he said. "I want you to go ashore and find Dr. Alvarez."

"I don't need a doctor," protested Steve.

"That's what you think," said Castignoni.

After breakfast the small skiff was launched. Randy, Louie and Freshwater dropped into it, the two younger fishermen taking the oars. The glassy harbor was dazzling in the morning sunlight, tinted in places with rainbow colors where there were oil slicks. The big Scandinavian, pretending he was an old-time bucko mate, harshly commanded them to set a stiff stroke. Randy and Louie grinned at each other, and by common consent slowed their beat until the skiff was barely moving.

"Mutiny!" bellowed Freshwater. "I'm going to lay it on

with my marline spike when I get you aboard the schooner, me hearties!"

They were halfway to the wharf when Randy heard the creak of more energetic oars. A heavily accented voice called across the water: "You are from *Reep-lay, verdad?*"

Forgetting his rôle of bucko mate, Freshwater asked in his normal tone what the man was saying.

Randy and Louie shipped their oars and turned to look at the approaching dory. The man rowing it was roughly dressed. His two passengers, however, were plump and stocky and had the prosperous appearance of wealthy *hacendados.* Clad in somewhat rumpled linen suits, and with straw hats set squarely on their large, round heads, their florid-brown coloring and broad, flattened faces suggested that they might be of Indian origin. But they had the black mustaches common to those of Spanish descent.

This puzzled Randy, for he had learned during his stay in San José that Costa Ricans were the only Latin-Americans with virtually unmixed blood lines. The Indian population of the territory had fled before the Spanish invaders. As a consequence, the settlers had become small landholders rather than big planters or *hacendados,* with many native laborers to work their estates.

Where did these men come from? the boy asked himself.

"He's pronouncing our boat's name as if it were a Spanish word," Randy explained to Freshwater. And raising his voice, he called in the other's tongue: "Yes, *señor.* We're from the *Reep-lay.*"

The man who had spoken now drew a newspaper clipping

from his pocket and unfolded it. A large diamond ring on his stubby hand flashed as he did so.

"You know *Señor* Var-doan?" he asked, after consulting the piece.

It suddenly occurred to Randy that clipping the man held was the account of his experiences which had appeared in the San José newspaper. The story had mentioned his flights with Steve.

"*Si, señor,*" Randy answered. "You'll find Steve Vardon on the *Ripple.*"

"*Mucha' gracias,*" said the man, folding up the paper.

Louie and Randy began rowing once more. As the younger boy was tying the skiff's painter to the wharf ladder, Freshwater spoke in a puzzled tone: "Now, why would those Costa Rican *jefe politicos* be wanting to see Steve?"

"They may be big government officials, Freshwater," said Randy. "But they're not Costa Ricans."

Leaving the big Scandinavian to watch the boat, the two younger fishermen walked into town. Dr. Alvarez was not in his office, but they found him at the hospital. He agreed to accompany them back to the boat.

They drew up to the *Ripple* a short while later and saw the oarsman of the dory pulling away. His two plump passengers bowed to the doctor, and he nodded in return. It was clear to Randy, however, that the pair in the rumpled linen suits were strangers to Dr. Alvarez.

Randy scrambled up the Jacob's ladder, leaned over to steady the doctor as he climbed aboard, and then led the way to Steve's room.

Through the open doorway came unmistakable sounds of mirth. Randy glanced inside. The navigator was reading the newspaper account that the stranger with the diamond ring had previously consulted. "Did you give the paper this wild yarn, Randy?" Steve chuckled.

The boy flushed. "Not that way, Steve. The reporter made some mistakes. . . . This is Dr. Alvarez."

Randy reported to the captain that the doctor was aboard, and then went to the galley where a number of fishermen were having a mid-morning snack. The boy scarcely had time to finish a second generous sandwich before Joe Castignoni came looking for him.

"Randy, row Steve and the doctor ashore. The doctor thinks that Steve should be X-rayed at the hospital."

"I'll come along," offered Louie.

Randy and Louie ferried the two men to the wharf and then waited until the noon sun was blazing overhead. Louie suggested that the navigator must have been kept at the hospital. They decided to return to the *Ripple* for lunch. They had taken only a few strokes when they saw Steve sauntering along the wharf. His head was freshly bandaged and he was whistling cheerfully.

"If you hurry," shouted Louie, "you can make it in two jumps."

"Back up," ordered Steve with a grin. "I'm in no shape to jump."

As he started down the ladder, there was a shout at the other end of the wharf: *"Señor! señor!"*

It was the two plump strangers, looking more wilted than

· 211 ·

before in the sweltering midday heat. Steve frowned slightly as he waited for them to overtake him.

Without a word, the man with the diamond ring removed a leather bag from his sagging pocket. He loosened the drawstrings to allow the American to peek into it. Steve's eyes rounded with astonishment. He appeared somewhat dazed as he watched the man pull the string and return the pouch to his pocket.

The other Latin-American now slipped a bulging wallet from his coat pocket and opened it sufficiently for the navigator to glimpse its contents before he replaced it in his pocket. Randy was sure that the wallet held an impressive amount of currency, for Steve whistled softly.

"Will you now believe that we speak the truth, *señor?*" asked the man with the diamond ring in Spanish.

"*Señor,*" said Steve emphatically, "I must offer my apologies for doubting your word."

"You will come with us then, *verdad?*"

Steve pushed back the cap on his bandaged head. His face had a far-away expression as he stared at the water. "I'll have to think about it, *señor,*" he said at last.

"We have lost much time trying to find a well-trained pilot. When we happened to see a copy of *El San José Diario* that mentioned some of your flying experiences, *señor,* we knew you were the man we wanted. Now we must know at once!"

The lines in Steve's face sharpened. "It won't be the answer you want," he said quietly, "but if you must know this minute . . ."

"It is not that urgent, *señor!*" the man hastily assured him.

"Then I'll see you later today," said Steve.

As Randy and Louie rowed back to the *Ripple,* the navigator must have noticed the boy's troubled expression.

"How'd you like to be my co-pilot, Randy? I might teach you enough about flying to take out a Nicaraguan license in a year or so."

"Were those men Nicaraguans, Steve?"

"Sure. I may go to work for them."

"I wish I could be with you. But I want to find Frank. We've always planned to fish together."

" 'Old Bulldog Randy'!" said Steve, laughing. "Once you get a grip on something, nothing can shake you loose. But I hope you find Frank."

They tied the skiff to the Jacob's ladder, and Steve went to his room. He remained there, apparently debating whether to accept the Nicaraguans' offer of employment, throughout the lunch hour.

During the meal, Tony Riggio spoke of the time an eruption of a Central American volcano had allowed chunks of pumice to drift down a river and out to sea. He declared that he and his mates had scooped up quantities of the porous material to use in polishing brass.

The story reminded Randy that the wheelhouse instruments were becoming tarnished and that it was his duty to keep them bright. So, after eating, he went up to the bridge with cloths and polish. He was hard at work on the gyrocompass when Steve appeared. The navigator gave him a mock salute, then knocked on the captain's door.

"Come in," shouted Joe Castignoni.

Steve opened the door and pushed back his cap. "Joe," he said, "I've decided to leave the *Ripple*."

Castignoni rose in surprise. "What's wrong, Steve?"

"Tuna fishing is too slow for me, Joe. Too much bad weather, too many fish that won't bite, too little change. I'm fed up."

Sadly Joe Castignoni shook his head. "Everything turns out that way for you, doesn't it, Steve?"

"So far," said the navigator, laughing. "But I keep trying."

"What have you got in mind?"

"Two Nicaraguans offered me fifteen hundred a month to fly ore from their gold mine in the southeastern mountains to Bluefields on the Caribbean coast. At present too many of their burro-trains are picked off by bandits."

"It might be fifteen hundred in empty promises, Steve."

"That was my first thought. But they showed me enough pure gold and American currency to choke a porpoise."

After a long pause the captain said gravely, "Where is this getting you, Steve?"

"I'm restless, Joe."

"Sure, sure—I know. As a kid I wanted to be a circus aerialist, but Vittorio made me keep on fishing. Now I've got a good boat, a nice home and money in the bank. You can have all that, Steve."

"I don't want to be tied down."

Castignoni sighed. "Every time you shift to a new job, you've squandered all the time you spent learning the last

· 214 ·

one. Did you ever take a good look at the down-and-outers on park benches—the men who frittered away their lives chasing rainbows?"

"You won't find me on a park bench!" Steve said brusquely.

"I won't argue, Steve," the captain said quietly. "I expected the day to come when you'd see greener pastures. But you have so much ability that I hate to see you rolling along the road to nowhere."

"You can't pin down a man with wandering feet," said Steve.

"If I can't appeal to your head, Steve, I'm going to appeal to your heart. Will you sail with us to the Galápagos Islands?"

Randy's heart gave a startled bound. The captain had appeared unwilling to consider the idea that the *Westwind* might be in the Galápagos archipelago. Apparently he had had a change of heart!

"Why would those islands appeal to my heart?" asked Steve, puzzled.

"Randy convinced me that my brother's boat might have been lost there. Her crew may even now be stranded on one of the islands."

Steve hesitated. "The Nicaraguans need me right away, Joe."

"Worse than I do?" demanded Castignoni. "When a whole crew may be starving on some barren rock or little isle? How could I find those men without a pilot for the plane? It would take weeks to explore every last dot of land thoroughly by boat and on foot!"

The navigator tipped uncertainly on the balls of his feet. Twice he cleared his throat as if about to speak, only to lapse into silence.

Randy stopped rubbing the gyro-compass with his cloth. He held his breath, while small, swift tremors shook his knees. Upon Steve's decision, he felt sure, hung the fate of the clipper *Westwind* and her crew!

CHAPTER THIRTEEN

Air Search in the Galápagos

IT SEEMED to Randy that the long silence would never end. When at length Steve Vardon spoke, his voice was edged. "You know I wouldn't leave you here, Joe, if there was any real chance of finding the *Westwind's* crew. But you yourself have argued that your brother couldn't have gone to the Galápagos."

Dull color crept into Joe Castignoni's face and his stocky body stiffened. Then he shrugged and said, "You think this is a trick to keep you from leaving the *Ripple*, don't you, Steve?"

"What else can I think, Joe?"

"I intended to return you to Puntarenas after you'd searched for the missing men," said Castignoni in a hurt tone.

"Sorry," said the navigator. "I should have known you wouldn't try anything underhanded, Joe. But what makes you believe now that the *Westwind* sailed to the Galápagos?"

Briefly the captain described Randy's efforts to discover how many oil drums were stowed on the *Westwind* and how his deductions made it seem unlikely that the clipper had been lost on the Central American coast.

Until now both men had seemed oblivious of the boy's presence. But when the captain finished speaking, Steve turned and doffed his cap. "The old maestro!" he said.

"Aw, Steve!" cried the boy, flushing. "I was trying to find Frank."

"Looks like you've given us a good clue," declared the navigator, an excited note in his voice. "Count me in, Joe!"

"What about the Nicaraguans and their mine?" asked Castignoni.

"I'll go ashore now and tell them I can't report for work until the *Ripple* returns from the islands."

"And what if they won't agree?" asked Randy anxiously.

"Then," said Steve cheerfully, "they can find another pilot."

With a wave, he strode out.

Steve was back from Puntarenas an hour later with a Costa Rican pilot. The *Ripple* immediately weighed anchor and set sail. She was well out into the gulf when the government launch came alongside and took aboard the pilot. Not long afterward the clipper was in the open Pacific, pounding through heavy seas on a southwesterly course that would take her to the Galápagos Islands.

On the morning of the fourth day after the *Ripple's* departure from Puntarenas, Randy was at the wheel, when he spied a mass of low-lying clouds, far across the deep-blue water.

"Are we heading into a storm, sir?" he asked the captain.

"From April to December, when the trade winds blow regularly, you seldom have gales in the Galápagos," the skipper answered drily.

And then, as if feeling he had been too curt, he added in a more friendly tone, "The coastal parts of the islands, up to eight hundred feet, have only a short rainy season from February to June, Randy. And from June to November the upper slopes of the islands are shrouded in thick mists, at least during the mornings. Like as not, there will be morning rains above eight hundred feet as well. Either rain or mist will handicap us in our search for the *Westwind*."

After another hour had passed, Randy saw that the clouds hanging over the Galápagos Islands had a peculiar shape, for they rose like a series of gray pinnacles. The explanation of this serrated formation came to him at noon, when the thinning mists revealed volcanic peaks heretofore hidden. Each of the larger islands that he could see appeared to have one or more volcanoes, though only the broken summits of several cones and the bases of the islands were as yet visible.

Knowing that this archipelago, or group of islands, lay at the equator, Randy had imagined the heat would be intense. Contrary to his expectations, the breeze blowing through the opened windows was soft and fresh. He commented on this, and the captain explained the contradiction.

"A cold Antarctic current sweeps northward along the South American coast to Peru, Randy, and then swings westward. At these islands it meets a warm current flowing southward from the Gulf of Panama. Where warm and cold currents clash, there's always mist or fog. You'll probably discover those currents for yourself it there's time for a swim. On the south side of some islands the water is a chilly sixty

FATE OF THE CLIPPER WESTWIND

degrees, while on the opposite side of the same islands it may be twenty degrees warmer."

The *Ripple* was soon drawing near San Cristóbal, the easternmost island of the group. It appeared to stretch over twenty miles across the blue sea, and though the northern end was parched and rocky, Randy observed that the southern coastline had dense vegetation. Through the golden sheen of haze, he made out volcanic peaks to the southwest, soaring perhaps half a mile above the ocean. Toward this mountainous end of San Cristóbal the captain ordered him to steer the vessel.

"We've got to put in to Wreck Bay," explained the skipper. "Then I have to hike four miles inland to show my papers to the Ecuadorian official at Progreso before we can take bait or fish. It's a blamed nuisance, but Progreso is the only point of entry in the islands."

When the boat was approaching the southern tip of the island, the captain took the wheel, but asked the boy to stand by. Randy could not see why he had been relieved. The sparkling blue water appeared perfectly calm. As the vessel rounded the extremity of the island, however, she began rolling in the heavy ground swells rebounding from the black cliffs. Presently they came abreast of a break in the coastline. Within this tiny cove, Randy saw two waterfalls plunging perhaps thirty feet down the rock walls.

"Freshwater Bay," Castignoni enlightened the boy. "The only dependable source of pure water in the islands. But it's a desperate skipper who will risk his vessel in these ground swells to fill his tanks!"

Scanning the sea ahead, Randy could soon see a long, whitish streak against the prevailing blue of the ocean—a submerged coral reef. He realized that it must be the hazard that had given Wreck Bay its name. Captain Castignoni chugged slowly past this pitfall and turned into the bay. It proved to be a snug though not impressive anchorage, its shorelines a heavy tangle of mangrove thickets. The few shacks to be seen along the beach were unpainted and weatherbeaten. On the hill above them, the captain informed Randy, was the only lighthouse in the islands. The "lighthouse" was nothing more than a gasoline lantern on a long pole, with a steel ladder by which it could be tended. The *Ripple* slowly drew to a stop off a shaky landing stage which appeared about to fall apart.

A dory, rowed by a brown-skinned youth, immediately put out from shore. In the stern, stiffly erect, sat a portly little man whose broad, mahogany-colored face was almost hidden beneath the visor of a cap several sizes too large. The tarnished gold braid ornamenting the cap suggested that its wearer might hold some official position, though he wore no uniform.

Freshwater lowered the ladder as the dory drew alongside, and the captain strode aft to welcome the visitor. The little man, with rigid dignity, climbed aboard.

"I am the Chief of Police," he proclaimed with a sweeping gesture. "I am the Governor of San Cristóbal. I am the Captain of the Port. I am the Keeper of the Lighthouse. I must see your papers."

The captain with difficulty suppressed a smile. It was clear

· 221 ·

that the pompous little fellow was the only Ecuadorian official on the island. Castignoni made the deep bow this occasion seemed to call for and handed the official the packet of papers he had intended to take inland to Progreso.

The Ecuadorian barely glanced at them. As they were made out in English, a language with which he was apparently unfamiliar, he merely bowed stiffly and returned the packet to Castignoni.

"All is well," he said in Spanish.

Although the little man's official duties were ended, he spent another hour visiting with the captain before he departed in the dory.

"He wasted a lot of time," grumbled Castignoni, starting forward. "But he saved me a hot, dusty walk to Progreso."

Without delay the clipper sailed from Wreck Bay. Leaving San Cristóbal behind, she headed northeastward past tiny Isla Santa Fé and into the lee of the much larger island of Santa Cruz, where it would be safe to launch the plane.

"May I go with you?" Randy asked as he climbed onto the canopy to help the pilot remove the tarpaulin.

"Why not?" asked Steve good-naturedly. "This was your idea."

Presently the plane was deposited on the water and Steve was revving up the engine. Then at last they were off, the pontoons clapping harshly until the craft broke surface suction and began to climb.

For a while Randy watched the silvery blur of the sunlit water streaming under the tilted wings. They were zooming into a brilliant sky. The sparkling sea began to flatten out with altitude. Randy was astonished at the great number of islands he could see.

Steve leveled out at ten thousand feet and began to circle. Seldom did he climb that high when looking for a school of fish. A tingle ran down the boy's spine. For the first time, he realized, they were making a flight for no other purpose than to find the *Westwind*.

From his study of the pilot book, Randy knew that the Galápagos Islands covered over three thousand square miles. To thoroughly explore such an area of sea by boat would take weeks. A visual search, at the altitude at which they were flying, could be made in little more than five hours. This raised in Randy the hope that before darkness ended their flight, they would find the missing clipper.

Eagerly he swept the sea with binoculars. He could see six large islands, nine smaller ones and countless tiny dots of land that were little more than great rocks sparsely covered with vegetation, or the tips of volcanic cones rising from the sea floor. From the pilot book he had also learned that there were two thousand volcanoes in the archipelago. He could now believe this was so; beneath the buzzing plane were numerous yawning craters. On the largest island—the Isla Isabela or Albemarle of the charts—there were six huge craters, the rim of the highest soaring nearly a mile above the sea.

Gradually Randy began to notice the amazing similarity of the islands, whether large or small. Except for the rectangular form of San Cristóbal and boot-shaped Isabela, they were all roughly circular. Usually there was a large volcanic cone in the center of each island and smaller ones along its flanks. Dense shrubbery or trees grew luxuriantly over the southern sides of many, where rain was dropped by the warm, moist trade winds. The northern portions of the islands were rocky and bare, save for a sparse growth of cactus and thorn trees.

Randy began to understand how difficult it would be for the *Westwind's* crew to survive on any of the smaller isles, for only on the larger ones could he see small herds of cattle, sheep and goats. He was sure livestock would have been placed on other islands if there had been sufficient water for the animals to exist.

Remembering how disheartened he had been when Steve had flown over the hatch cover on which he was drifting, Randy moved the binoculars constantly as the plane circled. Sunlight, glittering blindingly from the water, soon made it harder and harder to distinguish anything clearly. Long, submerged rocks bore a startling resemblance to sunken boats. Cattle, half-hidden in brush, appeared to be walking men. And the human figures visible near small clearings or unpainted shacks escaped his notice entirely until they moved.

As the sun touched the horizon, Steve taxied alongside the *Ripple* and shut off the plane's motor.

"Tough luck, Randy!" he said sympathetically.

"I haven't given up hope yet, Steve," the boy said doggedly.

While that was true, the search had shown Randy what an appalling task confronted them. They had made a visual

· 224 ·

exploration of the group at an altitude of nearly two miles. Now they must fly low, skimming along the shores of the islands, so that nothing unusual could escape them. A search like that would consume days! Captain Castignoni was only half-convinced his brother had sailed to the Galápagos, and he might not allow them enough time.

As luck would have it, the search was temporarily discontinued only fifteen minutes after the plane took off the following morning. Randy spotted a school of tuna led by a bounding line of porpoises. When Steve reported the discovery, the captain ordered him to circle until the *Ripple* could reach the spot.

Half an hour later the plane was taken aboard. The moment Doc Bernedetto began chumming, eager yellowfins were fighting for bait off the portside. They were two-polers, which meant that Randy and Louie were teammates. The captain's son was in such high spirits at being able to fish again, however, that the younger boy could not have asked for a more pleasant companion. Throughout the day the air remained balmy and the sea rolled with light, glassy swells. Thirty-eight tons of tuna were taken aboard by nightfall.

While the clipper sailed to a safe anchorage in James Bay, on the western side of San Salvador Island, the men stowed away the fish. The vessel was still under way after the last yellowfin was dropped into the well. It occurred to Tony Riggio that they were rounding the northern end of San Salvador and must be in the tropical Panama Current.

"Last man in is a landlubber!" he yelled, starting at a run for his room.

Randy joined the stampede of fishermen, although he had no clear idea of what they planned to do. But when he saw Louie pull a pair of bathing trunks from his locker, he understood. Soon every fisherman not on duty lay on one of the iron racks. Warm water splashed and rippled over their bodies as the clipper sped along. It was soothing after the strenuous work of boating large tuna. Randy had never enjoyed a dip so much.

That was to be the pattern of the days that followed. Shortly after sunrise Steve and Randy would take off in the plane. They would skim around the shores of eight to a dozen islands still shrouded in morning mists, and then one or the other would sight a school of tuna. Fishing would continue until the light failed, and then the men would have a cooling dip on the grilled racks.

It worried Randy to see the fish wells rapidly filling. He felt especially uneasy when the last of their anchovettas were transferred from the bait wells to the big wooden deck tanks. For the bait wells, like those used solely for tuna, were equipped with ammonia coils for chilling brine, and when they were stowed with fish there would be no more storage space left. Captain Castignoni would then feel impelled to sail for San Diego, whether or not the *Westwind* had been found.

This might have happened quickly but for one circumstance. Each day the clipper had sailed several times through the warm equatorial current into the cooler one reaching the islands from the Antarctic. The pumps constantly supplying fresh sea water to the bait wells and bait tanks were thus drawing in brine that was alternately warm and cold. These variations of temperature were hard on the chums. Doc Bernedetto would scoop out hundreds of dead anchovettas every morning. So heavy were their losses that all of the chums were gone, while most of the space in the last two wells was still to be filled.

Since this would delay them while they looked for bait, Randy could not regard it as a misfortune. He hoped that in his flights in search of small fish he might find some sign of the *Westwind*.

The hunt for bait, however, took far less time than usual. It was only an hour after Randy and Steve had set off in the scouting plane before the pilot noticed hundreds of pelicans and man-of-war birds circling over a cove on the lee shore of Isla Isabela.

Steve banked the plane and dived toward the inlet. While they were still several miles from this protected cove, Randy saw that the water was dotted with feeding pelicans. Man-of-war birds dived for small fish without alighting on the water. Steve immediately banked the plane and sped northward to be taken aboard the *Ripple*.

The clipper sailed southward and let go her anchor just within the entrance of the little inlet. The first set of the net was completed by the time the noon sun was ablaze overhead.

Riggio helped Randy into the aqua-lung dress, and the boy descended to purse the seine. Treacherous coral and the ridges of old lava flows made it difficult for him to draw the net together on the steeply pitched bottom. After a far longer time than usual, Randy had the net pursed and tied. He made

· 227 ·

a slow, spiralling ascent to avoid the bends.

The small fish were brailed into the bait tank, and a second set of the net was made in mid-afternoon.

Randy dived less than twenty feet to reach the upper portion of the seine, which was caught on a projection. He freed the snagged net easily enough. In clearing the bottom strands and drawing them together, however, his hands were badly cut on coral and lava. His work was nearly done when his air line suddenly constricted.

He flipped the lever on his tank to tap his emergency supply of air. With seven-eighths of his supply exhausted, he realized that he must work rapidly to finish before his air was all gone. As he toiled, he could see the shadows of the milling sardines above him playing across the black-and-white floor of the cove.

Randy thought the seine was ready to be pursed when he discovered that it was snagged in two places by coral heads. He was tempted to abandon the job temporarily while he ascended for a fresh tank of air. But he decided that he might be able to finish if he made the seconds count.

Kicking with his swim fins, he pulled himself along the bottom line toward the places where the webbing was caught. Suddenly he saw a dark shadow, like a submarine in shape, gliding swiftly across the floor of the cove. He was not sure as to what cast the shadow, but its great size indicated that a shark was diving toward him.

He had reached the first of the two coral heads. Now he made the mistake of swimming past it in the belief that the net would give him greater protection where it was stretched taut between the two coral formations. His heart faltered when he tried to raise the webbing and found it rigid. Yet somehow, from sheer desperation, he squeezed beneath it without ripping his dress.

Lying on his face, with his heart hammering, he turned his head. Through his face plate he caught a fragmentary glimpse of the white end of a pectoral fin and a long, cylindrical gray body. Although the creature vanished as quickly as it had appeared, Randy knew that what he had seen was a white-tipped shark—the fiercest shark encountered by tuna fishermen.

Through the gum-rubber hood of his dress, the boy heard two sharp claps—followed seconds later by four other reports.

The shark flashed by a second time, its caudal fin flailing the water into swirling eddies. The net jerked as the monster's tail struck it, but it did not break away from the coral to leave Randy exposed to attack.

He waited, breathing as lightly as possible to conserve the small amount of air remaining in his tank. When the shark failed to reappear, he decided that it must have left the cove. The .45-caliber shells Steve had fired into its body could not have done much actual damage, but they had apparently served to discourage the monster against making further attacks.

I must ascend in a hurry! Randy thought. *My air's almost gone!*

Starting to wriggle out from under the rigid net, he found that it held his back in such a tight grip that he was unable

· 229 ·

FATE OF THE CLIPPER WESTWIND

to move. He tore his hands pushing against the bottom. Still he couldn't budge! A chill of terror washed over him. His aqua-lung tank must be entangled in the webbing! Now, with his air almost exhausted, he was trapped on the floor of the cove!

CHAPTER FOURTEEN

The Secret of the

Bobbing Rock

RANDY TWISTED and wrenched to free the tank on his back from the net in which it was caught. This brought about an unexpected result. The bit he gripped between his teeth was loosened, and he swallowed a mouthful of brine before he could work it into place again. The straps supporting the tank also gave a little, though not enough to allow him any greater freedom of movement.

"If I keep struggling, I'll break my air connections," he told himself. *"Then I'll drown!"*

He lay quietly on the sea floor, trying to think what could be holding him. He decided that the little lever by which he released his reserve air must be caught in the seine. And pinioned down by the rigid webbing as he was, he couldn't reach it! He tried to turn over, on the chance that he might free the lever. Again the entangled tank defeated him. He couldn't move!

He was startled to feel something pulling at the net. Fearing that the shark had returned, he twisted his head to peer through his face plate and was astonished to see a brown-skinned swimmer, clad only in a pair of striped shorts. The diver was heavier and larger than Riggio. Randy turned his head a little more and recognized Louie Castignoni. Air bubbles streamed from between Louie's lips. And something in his hand streaked with dazzling flashes in the bright water.

Louie was slashing the webbing with a knife!

The captain's son had played a more positive role since his conversation with Randy at San José. Voluntarily he had taken the wheel half a dozen times on the cruise to the Galápagos and, while he was still an erratic helmsman, he was improving. And it was on his own initiative that he had bought the cream pitcher and sugar bowl for Randy's mother while shopping in Puntarenas. Despite these signs that Louie was trying to assume responsibility and make his own decisions, Randy would never have expected him to take the lead in a crisis of this kind.

Louie ripped and tore at the rigid webbing with his knife. Then, seizing the boy's arm, he jerked Randy partway out from under the net. Unable to hold his breath any longer, he sculled the water to drive himself upward.

Small fish, blazing silver in the luminous water, streamed through the parted seine to escape. And, like the fish, Randy discovered that he also was free. He had to fight down a temptation to streak to the surface. After so many minutes below, however, that might bring on the bends! Instead, he swam in slow spirals, kicking and flexing his arms, exhaling deeply to expel as much nitrogen as possible from his blood before the air was depleted in his tank.

Possibly a minute after starting his gradual ascent, air ceased flowing into Randy's mouth. No choice was left him but to kick hard with his fins and snatch off his face mask the moment he broke water. He paddled to the net skiff, and groped until his hand touched the gunwale. He clung there, gasping for breath, while dark specks whirled before his eyes.

When his vision cleared, Randy saw Louie treading water beside him. Weakly he patted his rescuer's shoulder, panting, "Th-thanks, Louie."

"Forget it," said Louie, grinning. "Anyone can fall overboard."

"You fell overboard!" scoffed Riggio. "You should have seen him, Randy. When we saw that you were caught in the seine, Louie peeled off his clothes, grabbed my knife and was over the side before I had my boots off."

"Look, Tony!" wailed Nicco Puccinelli. "Our sardines!"

Tony Riggio glanced over the side, then cupped his hands and shouted toward the circling speed boat.

"Steve, fetch my diving gear. We're losing bait!"

The navigator sped back to the *Ripple*. By the time he had returned with Riggio's diving outfit and a ball of twine, however, a third of their catch had escaped through the opening in the seine. Riggio descended, quickly freed the bottom line from the coral heads, and then closed the parted strands of webbing with twine.

It was not an impressive haul of sardines that Steve towed out to the clipper!

Pelicans were once more wheeling over the cove as the last of the chums were scooped into the bait tanks. Although it was well past the dinner hour, the boats went out to set the net for the third time that day. Randy had the comforting assurance of a fresh tank of air when he dived to secure the bottom line.

The pursed seine was hauled to the *Ripple,* but the tired men ate before they began brailing. Doc Bernedetto beamed as he cast the final scoop into the port tank hours later.

"That should give us all the chums we'll need while we're here."

Randy's heart sank. They'd soon be sailing northward— and nothing had been learned of the *Westwind's* fate! Yet he knew that only a failure to find tuna could keep them in the islands much longer.

This took even less time than Randy expected. Early the following morning, when the *Ripple* set sail, Jack Lucca went aloft for a look around before going to breakfast. He sighted a school of four-polers, and before dark the fishermen had taken enough tuna to fill the last well.

Everyone was exhausted from hauling aboard the big fish, so the clipper anchored for the night off a sandy beach in James Bay, the snug little anchorage on the western side of San Salvador Island.

Before daybreak the next morning Randy was awakened by the rumbling of the Diesels. Realizing that they were about to get under way, he dressed hastily and hurried up to the bridge. The captain and Steve were there drinking steaming cups of coffee.

"We're not leaving before we make one final search for the *Westwind,* are we, sir?" he asked anxiously.

He knew he had flicked a tender spot when the captain's

face clouded. "You and Steve have spent hours flying over the different islands," Castignoni said brusquely. "I don't see what more we can do."

Randy nodded, and walked slowly into the captain's room to look at the chart. He saw nothing at first through the mist that swam before his eyes. Then several isles on the northern edge of the Galápagos group caught his attention.

With a surge of hope kindling his spirits, he returned to the wheelhouse. "There are several islands to the north that Steve and I never flew over," he cried eagerly. "Isla Genovessa and Marchena and Pinta. . . ."

The growing sternness of the skipper's face halted Randy. Then, knowing that it was his last chance, he felt he must continue.

He choked down a lump in his throat, and said in a hoarse voice, "If we can make just one more flight over those islands, sir, I'll feel we've done everything we could. I'll gladly pay for the gas—out of my share from the fishing."

Slowly Joe Castignoni's face relaxed. He even smiled slightly.

"You're a stubborn boy, Randy. But you'll never pay for gas to search for *my* son!" He glanced at the navigator. "How about it, Steve?"

"Randy has a point, Joe. We haven't flown very close to those three isles. I'd like to see what we can find."

"Good," said Castignoni. "I'll shape my course for Puntarenas as we'd planned. You'll have no trouble locating the *Ripple*."

His words were like a dash of cold water, telling Randy

that the captain thought this final flight would be brief and without results. Yet the boy was grateful to be allowed to make it.

"Get the plane ready," said Castignoni. "I'll rout out the crew."

A short half-hour later William McDowd, operating the winch with his usual skill, set the plane down on the glassy swells. Steve taxied through the entrance of James Bay. The plane then began to spank the water, speeding across the blue-and-silver rollers until it was airborne.

Excitement quickened in Randy as the little monoplane roared deafeningly in its steep climb. This was his last search for Frank Castignoni, and no visible clue must escape him!

With the binoculars, he swept the glinting sea and studied the surf-laced shoal waters surrounding each rock and tiny isle they passed. Twice he spied wreckage and called it to Steve's notice. But when the pilot swooped low, they saw hulks that had lain rotting for years.

After flying possibly forty miles to the northward, Randy shouted, "What's that low, rounded isle off to our right, Steve?"

"That's Marchena," yelled Steve. "We'll circle it on our return."

A dozen or more miles farther on lay Isla Pinta, a smaller though a much higher dot of sea-girt land. A moderate-sized crater, strewn with slate-gray lava rocks and studded with cactus, spoke of its volcanic origin. Steve circled Pinta, but they could see no signs of castaways.

The chart had shown two other rocky isles, far to the north-west, but they lay to the westward of any course the missing clipper was likely to have taken, so Randy made no comment when Steve turned to the southeastward.

The plane was scarcely a thousand feet above the sea as they approached Isla Marchena minutes later. Randy saw little to distinguish it from countless other volcanic islands he had viewed from the air in recent days. Rounded in form, it rose no more than eight hundred feet above the surf, lapping in white surges upon the black beach on its northern side. An identation on the northwest corner appeared to offer safe anchorage for small boats. Framing this cove was a beach, like a horseshoe in shape, its eastern end terminating in high rocks whitened with bird guano.

Seeing nothing moving at that side of the island, Randy turned the glass toward the southern end. There, beyond the crater pitting the center of Marchena, the trade winds had provided enough moisture to raise a forest of dwarfed trees and shrubs. Unable to detect any sign of life in that direction, he brought the binoculars to bear on the approaching shoreline.

Randy was moving the glass slowly across surf and beach when he saw something moving below the high, whitened rocks. Almost instantly the whirling propeller shut out his view.

The boy's voice rose in a shrill scream: "Steve, one of those rocks seems to be rising and falling!"

"*What!*" exclaimed the pilot.

The plane was already over the island. Steve banked the

little craft in a turn. As it came about, Randy focused his glass on what appeared to be a long rock or reef lying perpendicular to the white pillars guarding the eastern entrance of the cove. The light surges washing over the submerged object were milky-green, but to either side the water was clear emerald. And then Randy's heart skipped a beat as he had a momentary glimpse of what lay beneath the foaming surges.

"Rising and falling rock!" Steve bellowed, above the roar of the engine. *"That's a boat!"*

"The *Westwind*, Steve?" the boy yelled in excitement.

"You've got me! Let's try for a better look."

Steve continued to circle. Then, for a few instants, the sea was glassy-still beyond the white rocks. Through the transparent water, Randy made out the superstructure of a boat and a shattered mast. The pole, in falling, had sheared through the scouting plane and bait-tank canopy and nearly through one tank as well. There it was wedged. Then a ripple of foam flowed across the sunken vessel to ruin his view. The derelict, being partially buoyant, bobbed sluggishly in the currents. At that moment the roof of the wheelhouse and the captain's room broke the surface. Ripples spreading from the disturbance once more hid the boat from Randy.

Steve whistled. "She does look like a bobbing rock when she rises," he conceded.

He turned on the short-wave radio and called the *Ripple*. Joe Castignoni's voice instantly crackled through the speaker. Apparently Louie was at the wheel again, and the captain was standing by for a call.

· 238 ·

"We've spotted a sunken clipper that appears to be the same size as our boat, Joe. She lies off the north side of Marchena. Over."

The captain's shout made the speaker rattle: "Can you see any of her crew on the island, Steve? Over."

Steve didn't answer for several moments. "Sorry, Joe— but we can't. However, we're landing right now for a look around. Over."

"I'll head toward Marchena, Steve."

"Roger," said the pilot, shutting off the radio.

Making a wide turn, Steve buzzed in low through the entrance of the cove. He set the plane down and taxied in to the black strand. Randy scrambled out, caught the line the pilot cast to him and splashed ashore. Then he pulled the plane up higher on the beach and secured the rope to a lava rock.

Peering around, Randy saw that the pelicans scattered by their landing were now circling or alighting. Except for these birds, the cove had a desolate and deserted air that depressed him. He shivered slightly.

Steve dropped to a pontoon and stepped ashore. He cast rueful eyes on the low, black bluffs and the curving beach of blackened volcanic shale.

"If there were anyone here . . ." Then he stopped abruptly, frowning. "Suppose you search to the east, Randy. I'll go the other way. If you should find any survivors, whoop like a Comanche."

Randy nodded, and started along the rough beach. Behind him he heard rocks sliding as Steve began his ascent of the bluff. The next time the boy glanced back, he felt uncomfortably alone at discovering that his friend had disappeared. Onward he plodded, carefully picking his way around lava boulders that would have slashed his shoes like a razor if he had climbed over them. He was acutely aware of the sober gaze of the long-beaked pelicans watching him from the water.

Randy was approaching the end of the strand when a lean, dark figure suddenly appeared from between two of the large rocks rising above the eastern point of the beach. Clad only in fragments of clothing, the fellow's long, unkempt black hair and dusky, emaciated body seemed to mark him as a savage—or as best a wild man who had abandoned civilized habits. He carried a lengthy spear.

Catching sight of Randy, the stranger waved the spear and uttered a piercing scream that chilled the boy's blood. And then the wild creature bounded toward Randy with the fleetness of a deer. Randy was too frightened to wait and discover what the other's intentions might be. The waving spear made him suspect the worst.

"Steve!" Randy screeched, taking to his heels.

His cry, echoing from the walls of the cove, seemed to mock him. And apparently it did not reach the pilot, for there was no answer.

Behind him, as he sprinted with a speed born of his desperation, Randy heard the click and clatter of shale and rocks. These sounds almost drowned out his pursuer's yells.

Randy grew more alarmed as the sounds in his rear grew louder. Fearing that the wild man must be overtaking him, the boy darted a backward glance. Before he could see how much closer the other had come, Randy stubbed his toe on a rock and went sprawling. The fall stunned him but, nevertheless, he tried to rise.

His knees collapsed from shock, however, when his pursuer screamed, *"Randy!"*

A strong hand grasped Randy's arm and pulled him to his feet. He glanced uneasily at the long-haired, sun-darkened figure. Not until the other's white teeth and black eyes flashed did recognition come.

"Frank!" he yelled, flinging his arms around his friend. "Gee, you gave me an awful scare!"

"Hey, you—you're cracking my spine!" Frank gasped, laughing.

Randy released his friend and stood back, looking at him.

"You're so thin and sunburned I'd never have known you! I hope—you're not the only survivor?"

Frank Castignoni laughed and shook his head. He dropped onto a rock, and Randy did likewise.

"Everyone is safe, Randy. The others are in camp on the south side of the island. There are a few trees over there to give us shade. Spear fishing is better on this side; that's how I happen to be here. I'm the only one who has had much luck taking fish that way."

"Doesn't look as if you've been overeating!"

Frank grinned. "We haven't. But water has been our worst problem. The trade winds deposit a little moisture in the hollows of the higher rocks on the south side. That's all we've had to drink."

"It's sure good to see you, Frank!"

"I'm not exactly unhappy to see you, pal," Frank admitted with a flashing smile. "I saw a plane circling around and waved to the pilot, but I guess I'm burned so black that I couldn't be seen against the rocks."

Randy pointed. "There's the plane. Steve Vardon and I were making one last search from your father's boat before we left the islands."

"Did you happen to see the *Westwind?*"

"Yes, that's why we landed."

Frank smiled wryly. "Everything went wrong after I called you from the Gulf of Panama, Randy. We heard storm warnings on the radio, and Uncle Vittorio sailed here to escape the blow. Static was so bad that we couldn't tell anyone of our change of plans, and as it turned out, that was plain bad luck."

"You were caught in the storm?" Randy asked.

"Just in the fringe of it," Frank replied. "But several heavy seas caught us the wrong way, and either cracked or twisted our shaft. The propeller sounded like a big cement mixer after that. Still, Uncle Vittorio thought we might make this cove, and put down a diver to make repairs.

"It was blowing like crazy when we approached the entrance—although you rarely have strong winds here at that time. We'd have made it to shelter, though, if the propeller hadn't stopped turning. Before we could let go the anchors, we were driven onto the seaward side of those big rocks and stove a hole in the bow."

"That's when the mast toppled, Frank?"

"You should have heard it! *Crash—boom—bang!* I

thought the *Westwind* was coming apart at the seams! The pole ploughed through our scouting plane and almost through one bait tank. The impact hurled the speedboat from its chocks, and it crashed through uncle's room to smash up our radio equipment. The crew was knocked about, too, but luckily none of us was seriously hurt."

"But you hadn't a plane or a radio to fetch help?"

"That wasn't all, Randy. The mast lay across the after-hatches, keeping us from reaching the tons of tuna in the wells, even after it grew calm. The falling pole did us another bad turn. It forced out the side of the starboard bait tank, and the planking jammed the net skiff tight against the rail. Only the small skiff was left, and to ferry everyone ashore in it took three trips. We saved a little time, though, by running through the surf to the other side of the point. The skiff is still there, pulled up behind the rocks."

"Hasn't the *Westwind* shifted position since she struck?"

"She can't," said Frank with a grin. "Uncle Vittorio was in the last party to come ashore. He saw his boat had drifted out a few yards after her collision with the rocks, and he insisted that the stern anchor be let go. The men thought he'd lost his mind, but they humored him, anyway. When the wind died down everyone except my uncle was surprised to see that the clipper was still afloat and at times bobbing into view. Uncle Vittorio got a diver and several other men into the skiff, and rowed out to her. The diver dropped over the side and put a line on the forward hawser. Then my uncle and the others hauled up the hawser, rowed inshore and made the big rope fast to the rocks. The boat is held in such a tight grip by her anchor chain and the hawser that she can't strike again. But here is the amazing part, Randy. The *Westwind* is floating, though she's in fairly deep water!"

Randy laughed. "Yes, she's buoyed up by 121 oil drums."

"A hundred and twenty-one! There are far more than that, though even my uncle can't remember exactly how many. He didn't stay in San Diego long enough to claim refunds on those he picked up last trip. It made our engineer wild when he had to climb over stacks of oil drums to check the after-wells or the brine coils."

"Those barrels will make it easy to salvage the *Westwind*."

"That's what Uncle Vittorio says. He claims it could be done with the plywood table-top from another boat's galley. It wouldn't be much of a job to soak the table-top until it's pliable enough to bend, and then send down a diver to nail it over the hole in the *Westwind's* bow. Probably canvas ought to be tacked over the patch for added protection. Then the boat could be pumped out to bring her up. Now that Dad's here, we can do that, and he can tow the clipper to a Panama drydock for repairs." Suddenly Frank's eyes widened. "Say, how do *you* happen to be sailing on the *Ripple?*"

"I had a hunch I could find you," Randy admitted with a laugh.

Frank's black eyes lighted. "We'll fish together as we'd planned! The two of us can keep Louie from getting out of hand."

Randy sobered. "I'm not worried about Louie. He's changed a lot. But I don't think I can sail again on the *Ripple*.

Your father seems to dislike me, Frank."

"Dislikes you?" Frank cried in astonishment. "Why, Papa likes you better than any other friend I have!"

"He's changed then." And the light faded from Randy's face. "I guess we'll have to forget our plan of fishing together on the *Ripple.*"

"Any time we will! I'm going to find out what's wrong!"

Hearing voices, the boys turned. Steve Vardon was leading a group of ragged men over the brow of the hill. The boys started along the beach to join the party.

As he drew near the men, Randy was shocked by their emaciated appearance. The older fishermen showed the effects of their privation even more than Frank. Vittorio Castignoni, in particular, was appallingly thin, but he still held himself erect in his tattered clothing.

Tears streamed down the old captain's wasted brown cheeks as he tottered forward and embraced Randy.

"Steve spoke—of your determination to find us," he croaked hoarsely. "None of us—will ever forget it, my boy."

Randy had always liked old Vittorio Castignoni. Now he was so touched that his eyes brimmed.

Each of the marooned men walked up unsteadily to shake his hand and thank him. Embarrassed by their gratitude, Randy kept protesting that he had really done very little.

But for a few minutes these castaways helped him to forget the thing that lay heavily on his heart: *having found Frank, their paths must now separate.* Regardless of what his friend had said, Randy was sure that for some reason Joe Castignoni was strongly prejudiced against him.

· 245 ·

It seemed a long time to the hungry, ragged men before the *Ripple* finally hove into sight and made a wide turn to sail into the cove. No sooner was the clipper anchored than Steve climbed into the little monoplane and taxied out to be taken aboard.

Skiffs were lowered then, and when they reached shore everyone crowded into the two boats. Minutes later there were shouts as the men clambered up the ladder, shook Joe Castignoni's hand, and then walked with wobbling legs toward the galley to eat. Old Vittorio was so moved when he embraced his brother, that tears streamed down his gaunt brown cheeks.

Randy and Frank were the last to board the *Ripple*. Joe Castignoni hugged his son warmly, and then held him at arm's length, his eyes growing moist as he saw how thin the boy had become.

"We'll have to put meat on those bones before I dare let your mother see you!" he declared. Pointing to the galley, where the *Westwind's* hungry men were shouting hoarsely, he said, "You'd better start now."

Frank laughingly shook his head. "I'd be trampled in that mob!" Then suddenly he grew serious. "There's something more important right now, Papa." Slipping one arm through his father's and the other through Randy's, he said, "Let's go up to the bridge where it's quiet."

Upon reaching the wheelhouse, Frank smiled at his father. "Papa, Randy and I had always planned to fish together on your boat."

His father's dark eyes glowed. "I could use you both, but

you'll have a stiff partner to keep up with, Frank. Randy's a good fisherman."

"There's only one objection, Papa."

"What objection?" cried the captain, startled.

"Randy thinks you don't want him on the *Ripple*."

"Don't want him!" exclaimed Castignoni, his eyes widening with amazement. "I couldn't be more fond of Randy if he were my own son!"

While Randy was flustered that Frank had brought this into the open, he was relieved to see the captain's astonishment. Clearly Joe Castignoni harbored no ill feelings toward him!

"I—I thought . . ." Randy faltered, and then made a helpless gesture. "You bore down so much harder on me than on the others. . . ."

"Ah!" said the skipper softly. "I see! I see!"

Suddenly Castignoni broke into a roar of laughter. He laughed till his sides shook. And then, drying his eyes, he walked over to rumple Randy's hair good-humoredly.

"I had reasons for being rough on you, Randy. . . . My wife, you know, has always found it hard to manage by herself. When both my boys were old enough to fish, she was left alone, with no one to settle what problems arose. She was as distracted as a child faced with something too big for it to handle."

The captain began to pace the wheelhouse, waving his hands as he so often had in the past when stirred by excitement.

"Someone had to stay with Mama. But I was a fisherman;

· 247 ·

it is all I know. So I talked with Mr. Giannissa, the president of the Italo-American Cannery Company where I deliver my fish. Giannissa smiled when I finished telling him my problem. 'Our assistant production manager retires in three years, Joe,' he told me. 'If your wife can stick it out by herself that long, you can have his job. I think you can handle it all right. And if you do, you'll be in line to become our production manager when he retires six years from now. It's a good job, at a good salary.' "

The skipper paused and pointed a finger at Randy.

"You see where that left me? I had a boat that brought a good income. I wanted to keep her and put her in charge of a captain I could trust when I went to work for the cannery. But who in my crew would accept such responsibility? Louie? No, he was too much like his mother. . . . Ortorio, Freshwater, Puccinelli, Riggio or Bernedetto? No, no! All these men would be overwhelmed with the problems of commanding a clipper! Steve? He was an able navigator, but he has never quite grown up. He dislikes heavy responsibility or any feeling of restraint. I was sure also that he would never remain a tuna fisherman very long.

"Then I thought of Frank. Even as a young boy, he could decide matters and was willing to take charge when necessary. Still I hesitated, because in three years Frank would be only nineteen. Yet other able men a year younger than that have commanded tuna clippers. So I made up my mind to give Frank a severe course of discipline in order to teach him everything that I know, all within the short space of three years. I had no objection when he wished to make his first cruise with his uncle, for there is no smarter fisherman than Vittorio. Then, on Frank's first trip, the *Westwind* was lost! I did not know what to do then.

"But when you came aboard, Randy, and reminded me of how much you and Frank were alike, I decided to train you in my son's place. I heaped work and responsibility upon you to see if you had what is required in a captain. It was severe, but you showed that you could take it without complaint. By the time Louie had to go to the hospital in Costa Rica, I had learned that I could depend on you and I felt you could take as good care of him as I could myself. In almost all ways you have pleased me, Randy. Sometimes it was difficult not to show that I felt toward you as a father does toward his own son. But that I could not do! A captain's course is a hard one. Only by preparing you for the problems ahead could I help you."

Randy had listened in amazement to Joe Castignoni's words. Now he had to swallow several times before he could speak.

"Thank you, sir. You told me when I first came aboard that you expected of me what you would of Frank. I—I didn't understand."

Frank's blithe spirits could be restrained no longer. He laughed and said, "Now where does that leave me? I guess Randy will some day be captain of this clipper. I'll have to be his navigator."

For once Captain Castignoni's dark, hawklike face was torn with indecision. There was warmth and affection in his dark eyes as he glanced from Frank to Randy and then once more at his own son. Randy respected the man too greatly to see him forced to a decision.

"I'd be happy if I could some day serve under a captain like—like Frank Castignoni," Randy said quickly.

The skipper laughed and slipped an arm around the shoulders of both boys. "We'll let the future decide that," he declared.

Frank laughed lightheartedly. "Whichever way it goes," he said, "Randy and I will be sailing together as we'd always hoped to do." His eyes sparkled as he smiled at his friend, and then started toward the galley. "Didn't I say we'd make a team, Randy?"